Islands In The Sea

the king walks in!

Book I

a romantic, prophetic, mystery novel

by

Joseph James

Islands In The Sea

the king walks in!

Book 1

a romantic, prophetic, mystery novel by

Joseph James

published by
VaryMedia

ISBN: 978-0-9982212-0-5
Second Edition

Shaft Of Light™
Joseph James and Janiece Elaine Hartmann

Visit us at:
DestinyPathOfLife.com & Joseph-James.net
ShaftOfLight.com

CONTENTS

ACKNOWLEDGMENTS

I would like to thank the true Author of the book, the Holy Spirit. The Lord has given me a gift to write and when it is flowing, it does so gracefully. I simply wrote that which He showed me in visions and also in what He spoke.

I also want to thank my wife, Janiece. You are a rose in my life, such a wonderful fragrance of love. This journey with you has been nothing but miraculous as we have experienced so much of His goodness. Thank you for being committed to the journey. It has been a while now, but I feel like we have only just begun.

To all of my children and grandchildren, it is my hope that you can grasp this wonderful inheritance that is all yours. It is deeper than earthly riches could ever be, but it is far more valuable. May you take it and go further than us. It is yours to take to the next generation.

To all of our friends and family, thank you for believing in and encouraging us. I have heard it said that no one is an island unto himself. That is so true. We need each other and that becomes even clearer in the pages of this book.

There is no better life nor adventure than to walk each day in His Kingdom. Your Kingdom come, O Lord.

Joseph James

INTRODUCTION

"Islands In The Sea: The King Walks In!" encapsulates some prophetic visions into a fast moving, romantic story. While emphasis is given to the prophetic word, the story line uses descriptive elements to paint the images of the visions as well as give the reader a broader scope in its understanding. The interweaving of the story enables the reader to grasp the complexities and seriousness of the times we live in and to help understand how one person can make a difference in our world today.

Who is Dan? He's just a businessman who owns his own design and publishing company. Why is he chosen instead of those around him who are better qualified for the mission? What depths will the enemy go to stop him from spreading the prophetic dreams he has been given? Will Dan succeed or succumb to the fears in his heart? Enter his beautiful co-worker, Susan, onto the scene and things really get complicated. Is she strong enough to help him in the situations he is destined to face or is it going to scare her away and leave him all alone?

The setting is in our modern day and the place he lives is just an average city in the United States. Was this all just mere coincidence, or have the players and circumstances been carefully arranged for such a time as this. How could such an extraordinary plan be implemented in such a short period of time? Dan goes from a person in obscurity to a public figure almost overnight. What is the purpose and how will the plan unfold? How will the world react to the coming news? Who will heed the warnings and become those who arise in victory? It may not be the ones you think.

Joseph James

Chapter 1

A Nightmarish Night

Dan awoke with a jolt, his body was wringing with sweat. "Was it real?" he thought. "No, it must have been a dream! I have to get some sleep. I've been tossing and turning all night. It is already 4:15 and I have to get up at six o'clock."

Moments later his alarm sounded and he turned over and shut it off. *"Wow! What a night! I am so glad it was just a dream, but it seemed so real. Now I must get on with reality."* He tried all morning to get the dream out of his mind, but the dream kept haunting him. *"What did it mean? What was all that water and where was I?"* The dream was so far fetched that he couldn't have believed in it at all except that it felt so real, like he was really there. He had to tell someone. He had to share it before it overcame him. *"I know, I'll tell John. He'll tell me what I need to do."* John was always deciphering dreams for people. He seemed to have a God-given gift to understand the symbols and how they played out. The only problem was that today was only Tuesday and he would not see his brother until the weekend, but by then it might be too late.

His business demanded so much concentration and he just couldn't seem to focus. It just didn't seem as important as understanding this dream. "What could it mean?"

"Dan!" called Susan.

Shaking himself out of a stupor, Dan replied, "Yeah!"

"What are you doing?" asked Susan.

"What do you mean? asked Dan.

"You have been staring into space for the last twenty minutes. Has something happened? Do you need to talk?" asked Susan.

"No, it's just a crazy dream I had last night. I'll be all right." said Dan, not wanting to share the details of the dream. He didn't understand it himself so how could Susan help? She was always so quiet and kept to herself, yet she seemed really sensitive and attentive to her surroundings.

"Are you sure? I can listen. I'm pretty good at that." said Susan, hoping to find out a little more about Dan. She really admired him and the way he kept himself. He was really a quiet and soft spoken person, yet he had a way of gaining respect from everyone around him. I guess you could say that he had a sense of destiny and one could see that he was going somewhere and that somewhere was going to be a good place to be. She definitely hoped that she would end up there also. He was also very good looking. He was just over six feet tall, had dark brown hair, blue eyes and a medium frame. She really wanted to get to know him better. How could she convince him to share his dream with her without being too forward?

Was this really the right thing to do? Could he really trust Susan? She was really energetic all of the time. She was about five feet eight with long blonde hair and hazel eyes. Her body was toned and firm. Everything about her portrayed a picture of dedication to whatever she set her mind to do. It was a long time until Saturday and he could really use a friend right now. "Are you free for lunch?" asked Dan hesitantly.

"Yes! I am! That would be wonderful!" exclaimed Susan. Hopefully it didn't look like she was too eager. "It would be good to get my mind thinking about something else right now. All I'm seeing are questions in this layout and I don't have the answers yet."

"How would you like to go to Sally's Diner?" asked Dan. "They have a really good lunch menu. You can walk with me if you like."

"I would be glad to go with you. Let me get my sweater, sometimes it gets a little cool in restaurants," said Susan.

"Yeah! I know what you mean," Dan replied as he reached for his jacket, too.

As Dan and Susan walked the two blocks to Sally's Diner, they talked about how their paths had crossed. They found that they had a lot more in common than they thought.

After they had been seated and ordered their lunch, Susan asked Dan about the dream. "So what kind of dream did you have that is spacing you out so much? It must have been one of those dreams where you feel like you are actually in the dream."

"It is definitely one that had me tossing and turning in my sleep. I am still sleepy," said Dan with a yawn. "It all started out in the dark of night with a full moon out. I was taken up to the top of this dark, ominous, rocky mountain top. From there I was able to see a vast ocean with islands dotted here and there in the reflection of the silvery moonlight. They all appeared to be made of rock and were sticking up above the water."

"The next thing I saw was a huge rocky mass over to the left side of the sea. It was enormous and consisted of many smaller rocks pieced together. As I continued to watch, the huge mass began to rumble and vibrate. As it did, the rocks on the edge began to fall off into the sea. As I was pondering over the whole situation, I saw a huge swirling storm over the rocky mass. It looked like a giant hurricane except that it was over the land. Both of these things together were causing great destruction," said Dan.

"What was so bad about that?" asked Susan.

"Well, nothing at first, but then I noticed that all of the rocks appeared to be alive and breathing," added Dan. The rocks on the edge were trying to stay on top of the mass, but they kept getting pushed off by those next to them. I felt an emotion of tremendous anguish and pain as each rock hit the water. It was as if there was great sorrow in my heart every time one of them fell."

"But weren't they just rocks?" asked Susan with a grimace.

"It seemed that way, but the anguish I felt was real. It was overwhelming and I couldn't get away from that feeling. Even now, it seems like I have just awakened from it," replied Dan. The anguish and pain he was feeling was very evident on his face.

Susan was very concerned. "What do you make of it? What do you think this represents?"

"I don't know," said Dan. "My brother is the dream decipherer. Well, I guess that is a word. Oh well, it will have to do. I figure I will ask him about it on Saturday, if I can last that long."

"What are you going to do until then?" asked Susan.

"I really don't know. It is hard for me to concentrate on anything else. I may have to take off of work until I can get a grip on this situation. I really don't know," repeated Dan. "This hasn't happened to me before."

"Well, I will help you as much as I can on the project, but the deadline is coming up in two weeks. Hopefully, we can find the answer before then," said Susan.

"Are you sure about that? I'm not sure how I am going to get through this or how long it will take. I can't ask you to do that," exclaimed Dan.

"You're not asking me and I am not taking no for an answer," replied Susan rather enthusiastically. She hoped she wasn't too outspoken, but she knew he needed her help right now. "I guess we better get back to the office. Why don't you grab your things and take off for the rest of the day? I will get Jesse to look at the project and see if it is something we can let him handle for now."

"Okay." agreed Dan. He really wasn't feeling like putting up any additional resistance at this point. He was really tired and a good nap might be just the thing he needed.

"Do you mind if I give you a call later to check up on you?" asked Susan, hoping that he would let her. She was really feeling close to Dan. She had some bad relationships in the past with other guys and had been hesitant to reach out to anyone else, but somehow Dan was different. He was not like any of the crowd she was familiar with hanging around. She liked helping others and she was determined to at least give this her best effort.

"Sure, that would be great. I think I might like to talk to someone later this evening. Maybe we can meet for an evening snack. I know this wonderful little café that is kind of secluded and quiet. They have a patio out back with a waterfall and flowing stream. It's a wonderful place to sit back and relax. The sky is brilliant at night with the moonlight and stars," replied Dan. He really didn't want to be alone at all right now. He welcomed having company for a change. He'd gotten too familiar with being alone.

"Now, that sounds great. It has been a long time since I have taken any time to just relax. You have got yourself a date," exclaimed Susan. "I will call you later."

Chapter 2

The Mysterious Adventure Continues

Dan arrived home a while later and was ready to go to sleep. He dropped everything in the front room on his way back to his bedroom. He took off his clothes and fell into his bed. His head had barely touched his pillow before he was sound asleep.

All of a sudden there was a deafening roar and crashing waves. "What was that?" exclaimed Dan.

"That, my friend is the result of pride," said a stranger next to him. The stranger was clothed in a dark gray shirt and pants. The moonlight provided an outline of his silhouette. "Allow me to introduce myself. My name is Alex."

"Where am I and where did you come from?" asked Dan. He was visibly shaken up over the scene before him.

"Don't you remember me the last time you were here?" asked Alex.

"No, I don't! Am I supposed too? I was taken up to this mountaintop and was all alone," replied Dan rather insistently.

"Well, I am sorry about that. I thought you noticed me next to you," stated Alex apologetically. "I meant to introduce myself to you then, but you left so suddenly I didn't get the chance. I am glad you came back though. There is a lot more for you to see before you go back. I have been assigned to show you some things that are to come."

"What do you mean things that are to come?" asked Dan inquisitively.

"You know, future events," said Alex matter-of-factly. "There are some things you need to know so you can tell others before it is too late."

"Too late for what?" asked Dan seriously. "I don't even know what this is all about. It looks like a bunch of rocks and water to me, with the exception of what I am sensing."

"Everyone has a destiny and a purpose in their life. No one can survive as an island unto themselves. To a certain degree, everyone's life is changed by each person they meet, some for good and some for bad," said Alex.

"Well, that is understandable, but what in the world does this have to do with me?" asked Dan. He was trying to figure out why he was chosen for this task. *'Why not choose someone who understands all of this? Go figure,'* he thought.

"Dan you were chosen because of who you are and also because of choices you have made in your life," explained Alex.

'What's this? This guy can even read my thoughts,' thought Dan.

"No, I can't read your thoughts, but the Lord can and he has revealed some of them to me" exclaimed Alex so matter-of-factly. "I, my friend, am an angel and I have been sent to help you. Now that you are up to speed, how about we get on with this. There is a lot that I must show you and there is not much time."

"Okay," said Dan. It was at this point he realized that this was more than a dream. "So, what do we do next?"

"First of all, do you understand what you are looking at?" asked Alex.

"No, I don't, and I am very confused about what I see and feel. At times it is very overwhelming and it is the only thing I can think about," replied Dan seriously. "What is all of this and what are all of these rocks?"

"What do you see from here?" asked Alex.

"I see a vast expanse of water that seems to extend beyond my sight. I see some rocky islands protruding here and there above the water. Some of the islands are connected to each other and some are by themselves. I also see a large area of land that seems to have a lot of rocks on it. The shaking and storms seem to be moving the rocks around and some of them are falling into the sea," replied Dan. "There are also other structures rising above the water in other areas, but they seem to crumble back into the sea when the big waves hit them. There seems to be a lot of turmoil and unrest."

"Indeed there is," said Alex. "Everything is being tested right now. Every person's belief system, as well as community belief systems are being tested. Only the truth will stand. Everything else will fall."

"But what does all of this represent?" asked Dan. He was so troubled by what he saw and felt.

Suddenly, a fire truck went down the street in front of Dan's home and he awoke out of a deep sleep. He was glad in a way, to be away from the dream but he found himself wanting to really know what it all meant. He still didn't know for sure if it was a dream or something that was really happening in the spiritual realm. A short while later the phone rang and he went to pick it up. "Hello!"

"Hi, it's Susan. How are you doing?" she asked.

"I am doing much better," said Dan. "You have good timing. I just woke up a few minutes ago to the sound of a siren. How would you like me to pick you up so we can go to that café I was telling you about?"

"That would be wonderful. I have been waiting for this all afternoon," said Susan. She had hoped Dan would be up to going out this evening, especially after the way he looked earlier.

"Okay, great! I will pick you up at six o'clock if that's good with you." suggested Dan. This would give him some time to regroup and get a shower.

"Sure, that sounds great," replied Susan with excitement in her voice. "I will see you then."

"How do you like it?" asked Dan in reference to the patio scene behind the El Serena Café where they had just sat down.

"I love this. This is wonderful. It is so peaceful and calming here," replied Susan. The sound of the waterfall and running water provided a nice romantic setting. "I could get used to hanging out here more often. How did you find this?"

"I have a friend who told me about it. He was always telling me about how stressed he got and that this was one of his favorite get-a-ways," said Dan. "I have been coming here often since he brought me here one day. I guess it has been about two years now. It helps me to relax and remember that there is someone bigger than all my problems. Sometimes this man-made jungle of a city gets to looking too big and then I remember the streams in the mountains I used to visit and how much bigger God is. It helps me to keep things in perspective."

"I see what you mean," said Susan. "We used to live on the coast with the mountains close by. Every morning I would walk down the beach to the cliffs that overlooked the sea. I would look up at the waterfall off the mountainside as it cascaded down into the sea. It was so majestic, magnificent and so peaceful.

"Why did you move?" asked Dan.

"My dad was transferred to another city," said Susan. "We were all sad when we got the news. It was such a wonderful place to live. But enough about me, what is going on with you?"

"Well, I had an extension of the dream from this morning. As soon as I drifted off, I found myself right where I left off, but this time there was someone else with me," began Dan. He proceeded to tell her the dream as he remembered it.

"That is interesting, any ideas on what it means?" she asked.

"No, but I do have more questions and I am more at peace about it now," said Dan. "I also want to find out more about this angel."

"Do you think he is an angel or a demon?" asked Susan.

"I'm not for sure, but I will find out," said Dan. "I don't like playing games and if this is not on the up and up, it's going to stop real fast. I just hope it continues long enough so that I can figure out what the message is."

"This is really intriguing. Will you let me help you with this?" asked Susan. "I would really like to help you and help solve the mystery if you don't mind?"

"Sure, I don't see any reason why you can't," said Dan. "I think it would be great to have some help. You are a really special person. Thanks." They stayed at the café for a good while enjoying each others company. Dan took Susan home and then went back to his home. That night when he fell asleep, he went right back into the dream.

"Well, there you are!" exclaimed Alex as he saw Dan reappear. "I was beginning to wonder if you were going to come back."

"Yeah, I am here, wherever that is," replied Dan. He had really wanted to do a little more research about some questions he had before getting back to this dream, but time had run out and here he was again. "Okay, what now? By the way, how do I know that you are an angel of the Lord? The scriptures say that even the enemy masquerades as an angel of light."

"Well, the first reason is because I acknowledge the Lord Jesus Christ and am His servant. And the second reason is for you to decide. You must weigh everything I say and show you against His Word and the witness in your spirit," said Alex. "If it doesn't line up, don't believe it. However, if what I am saying is true, then you would do well to follow my advice."

Dan felt his heart skip a beat as he suddenly

realized the severity of his situation. This wasn't going to be something he could just pass off if it became uncomfortable. He could choose to walk away, but suddenly he was aware of what it would cost him. He started shaking and then his legs gave way under him as he crumpled to the ground.

Alex reached out his hand and touched him on the shoulder. Dan immediately felt a tremendous amount of energy flood his being. Suddenly he had the strength to stand up again.

"Come over here with me," said Alex. "There is more for you to see."

Dan had not felt this good in years. He felt as if he could fly if he chose. "Wow, this is great. It feels like my feet are barely touching the ground," he exclaimed. "What is over there?" He was pointing beyond the place where Alex was standing.

"This, my friend, is why you are here," said Alex. "Look at the huge land mass and tell me what you see."

"It looks massive and strong, but now I am able to see the supporting structures and some of it is crumbling," said Dan. "Also, there is a lot of shifting of the different sections."

"Good! That is what I wanted you to see," said Alex. "Time is running out. This massive structure is fixing to crumble."

"But what does it represent?" asked Dan. He knew somehow that he was to help, so he was trying to understand what he was seeing.

Alex began, "The sea represents all of the years through out the ages. The structures that rise up above the water and look like only the shells are left, are the kingdoms of the past that have risen to great heights. The kingdoms themselves have long perished, however some of their teachings and concepts still remain in some people's belief systems. The islands you see, are places in time where certain truths and revelations were given to the Lord's people. The massive structure you see over to the left represents the current day and age where many groups of people are fighting to build their kingdoms."

"Why is there so much more going on in this present time and not in the centuries past?" asked Dan.

"I'm sorry, Dan," replied Alex. "I have to leave you for now. We will begin where we left off at another time. There are things you must see and do in the meantime before we can get back together."

"What do you mean? How will I know what to do?" asked Dan. Once again, Dan felt weak.

"Go the way of peace, my friend. His peace will guide your feet. His love will embrace you and His grace will enable you to accomplish everything you will need to do," said Alex as he again put his hand on his shoulder.

Dan felt the power return as Alex touched him.

Dan awoke from his dream at the sound of his alarm going off. *'Wow, what a night,'* he thought. *'I have to get myself together so I can concentrate on work. Too much to do and seemingly not enough time to do it all.'* He was beginning to get totally stressed out.

It was then he remembered the words of the angel, *"Go the way of peace. His peace will guide your feet. Lord, help me to always remember these words. Thank You!"*

Chapter 3

A Day Of Questioning

Dan arrived at work early the next morning. He had seen Susan walk into her office, so he decided to stop by and say hello. "Hi lady! How are you today?"

"Good morning Dan," Susan exclaimed with a smile. "I am so glad to see you. I was real concerned about you last night, but you are looking great this morning." Then she added real quickly, "Tell me what has happened. Did you see any more? How was it?"

"Woah! Slow down a bit," said Dan. "I have to get back on the project for now. Jesse called last night and left a message while we were gone. He is not going to be able to do any more work on the project because of a situation that came up unexpectedly and he has to take care of it, immediately. Would you like to get together again this evening?"

"I would love to. Can we go back to the El Serena Café?" asked Susan. "I really like that place."

"Sure, how about I pick you up at seven o'clock?" asked Dan.

"That sounds greats. What a long time to wait," Susan said with a smile as she drew out the word 'long.' "You sure know how to keep a gal waiting in suspense." She was ecstatic. Yesterday, she had barely known anything about Dan outside of work, but after last night she felt a tingling sensation inside when she saw him. She hoped this was only the beginning of something great and lasting.

Dan found himself being able to concentrate on his work today. He was able to get things done faster than he had before. Everything seemed to be falling into place.

Then around three o'clock Susan stuck her head through the doorway. She seemed really distressed. "Did you hear the news?"

"What news?" he asked quickly.

"There have been two terrorist attacks today, one in London and one in Miami," she replied. "They have not released any detailed information, but they have increased the terror alert level."

"Was anyone hurt?" Dan asked as he got up from his desk to walk over to her.

"We don't know yet, but it sounds very serious. They have put other cities on alert," she replied as she walked over to him.

Dan held her close as she put her head on his shoulder. She was really shaken up. After she had settled down some, Dan asked, "Why don't we go to the conference room and see if we can get some more information?" He immediately thought of the dream he had and wondered if the events of today were somehow connected.

They walked over to the conference room, where everyone else had gathered. The reporter was just starting to give an update on the situation when they walked through the doorway. "A high rise hotel in London and one in Miami were hit today," the reporter said. "It appears that terrorists drove through the front doors of each hotel and released chemical agents inside by detonating some type of explosive devices. Emergency teams have responded to the scenes, but have been delayed until they can determine what kinds of chemicals have been released. They have not been able to determine how many casualties at this point and have asked all guests to stay in their rooms until emergency crews can assess the situation and determine a plan of action. No group has claimed responsibility at this time. We will bring new updates as they become available."

Dan stayed with Susan for a while after they went back to her office to make sure she was okay. Then he went back to his office and sat down just amazed by what they had just heard. As he began to think about what he had seen in the dream and the news he just heard. He also started thinking about other events that were happening around the world. There are wars here and there. The stock market is having its share of troubles. There is massive flooding in various areas. Earthquakes are becoming more frequent. Then there are areas experiencing great droughts. Governments are hurting their own people. Corporations are falling because of greed and criminal activity. Even government representatives are being exposed for all of the corruption in their lives. Laws are being passed that are infringing on people's individual rights and freedoms. Big corporations are becoming monopolies again. Drugs are being promoted more and more, even those with dangerous side effects. Children are killing each other. Crime is rampant. Gangs and turf wars are taking over some areas. If you turn on the news channels, mostly all you see are all the bad things that are happening. There are so many activists organizations around that it is impossible to determine which one is the better choice to join. *'How does this all fit?'* he thought. *'How is it all going to end?'*

He tried desperately to put all of this out of his mind so that he could concentrate on his work. Finally, the clock showed five o'clock. At last, he could go home and then spend a wonderful evening with Susan. He was really enjoying her company.

Dan arrived at Susan's place at six fifty-five. He was all excited about his new relationship. He even skipped a step as he walked up to her front door. As he put his hand out to ring the bell, the door opened and Susan appeared in the doorway. "Wow, you look lovely this evening," he exclaimed as he moved aside so she could exit through the doorway. She had let her hair down and it was flowing over her shoulders as the gentle breeze lifted it. Her eyes were sparkling in the glimmer of the slowly sinking sun.

"You don't look so bad yourself," she replied teasingly. "I was wondering when you were going to show up," she continued with a smile.

"What do you mean?" he asked jokingly, while playing along with her. "I was here five minutes early."

"Well, that may be so, but I have been waiting for this moment since this morning," she replied as she suddenly turned around to face him.

Dan had to stop in his tracks to keep from bumping into her, but as he stopped she advanced with her arms out as she jumped towards him. He caught her and they embraced each other. She continued, "I am so glad to be with you. Will you just hold me for a moment? I feel safe and at peace when I am with you. I have not felt this way with anyone else."

Dan hesitated for a moment. This was unexpected and yet it was so natural. He was totally enjoying the embrace. Her hug felt great and he did not want to stop just yet. "Thanks," he replied. "Don't let go yet. What took us so long to get together? We have been around each other for so long." He grabbed her firmly at the waist as he lifted her up and swirled her around. Her hair lifted in a blur as they went around several times before he let her down. They were having so much fun and neither one wanted to interrupt the moment, so they just held on to each other for what seemed a long time.

"Well, I don't know about you, but I am getting hungry," said Dan with a smile.

"Me too," replied Susan. "Let's go."

After they had finished eating, they sat back and relaxed in their chairs. They had talked about their families and how they were raised as kids. The evening was beautiful. The moon had begun to shine and only the deep shades of purple in the sky was all that was left of the sunset behind the mountains. The air was getting a little cool, so Susan grabbed her sweater and put it on. "Do you mind if we go over to my place? I have a wonderful little fireplace we could sit by as you tell me what is going on with you. I can't believe you have not said a single word about it."

"Okay, I guess we can do that," he replied. "Are you sure you don't want to wait until tomorrow?" he asked with a grin.

"You are really pushing it, buddy!" she exclaimed as she gave him a push towards the door.

After they had gotten settled at Susan's place around the fireplace, Dan began the conversation. "All right lady, so what do you want to know first?" he asked.

"Oh, how about everything from start to finish." she suggested.

Dan brought her up to speed on his dreams and the meeting with Alex. He also told her about the events he had thought of during the day. "I am thinking that somehow all the terrorist attacks have to do with everything moving around, and all the floods, earthquakes and storms have to do with the hurricane type storm I saw. That is what I am going to tell Alex the next time I see him."

"When do you think that will be?" she asked.

"Hopefully, tonight," he replied with a lot of enthusiasm.

Chapter 4

Terror In The Night

That night, Dan was awake most of the night. When he was able to sleep some, it was only in short spurts. He wrestled with all the events of the past two days and nights. How did he fit into the scheme of things, he wondered? And what about Susan, how did she fit in? How could the last two days be so wonderful and so terrible at the same time? The dreams kept playing over and over in his mind along with the terrorist attacks and all the other news. Finally, he was able to sleep for a short stretch of time.

"Alex, where are you?" Dan asked in complete terror. He was on the edge of a precipice, partway down from the edge of a cliff. It was about twenty feet to the top and the ocean waves were crashing against the rocks approximately 120 feet below. "Where am I?" he cried out. "Alex! Alex! Help me!"

It was then that he heard a voice in the wind,

"You are mine! All mine!" The raspy sounding voice seemed to be coming from right in front of him, but all he could see was a dark silhouette about 10 feet over to the side on another ledge. "There is no where to go but down and you are all alone. Let go and fall and it will all be over. Trust me. No one can save you now! You have gone too far and said too much. You have enemies."

"Who are you?" asked Dan as he trembled inside.

"My name is Terror and I have come to stop you," the demon said in a crackled, raspy voice. "You need to give up now. You don't have what it takes. Just who do you think you are?"

"What do you mean? Just what is it that I am doing?" Dan asked sheepishly as his voice came out somewhat garbled.

"You are trying to mess things up and I can't allow you to do that," replied the demon.

All of a sudden Dan awoke from the dream. His body was still shaking from the fright. "What was that? Man, this dream stuff is getting serious," he exclaimed under his breath.

"Well, if you think that it was a dream, you better think again!" exclaimed the same voice he had heard in the dream. Only this time the voice was coming from the foot of his bed. Then he saw a dark bony finger point at him from within the mass of darkness at the foot of the bed. "You are mine!" the voice said with a shout. "I have come for you!"

Dan was really shaking now. His whole body was noticeably trembling. He tried to speak, but his mouth would not move. Finally, after a few moments, he was able to whisper, "Help! Help me, Jesus!" He said it again, this time louder, "Help me, Jesus!"

All of a sudden the room was filled with light. Alex appeared in glowing splendor. Dan looked around, but the demon was gone. He was perplexed. "What is going on, Alex?" asked Dan as his body shuddered.

"It is a battle for your mind. You didn't think this was going to be a walk in the park, did you?" Alex asked seriously. "There is a battle being waged for every living soul. People die, some get hurt, and some just walk away. The spiritual world is real whether you can see it or not."

"I don't like this," replied Dan. "I sure didn't expect this."

"So, what are you going to do now?" asked Alex. "You, my friend, like every one else, are on the battlefield. You have a choice and that is choosing which side you are going to be on."

"What if I don't want to be on any side?" asked Dan.

"There is no middle ground," Alex began. "Your

life is a book. Others read it every day. You either draw people towards the Lord or help push them away from Him. Even if you don't make a choice, that in itself is a choice. The enemy does not care if you choose to help him or to do nothing. His job is still the same, 'steal, kill and destroy.' If you are not moving forward or standing your ground, you are going backward. It is your decision."

"What do I need to do to keep this from happening again?" asked Dan.

"There is nothing you can do to keep this from happening. However, it would be good for you to pray and walk with the Lord. He will keep you and protect you," replied Alex. "That is one reason I am here. Now, let's get on with this revelation."

"Revelation?" asked Dan curiously.

"Yes. I am here to reveal something to you that has been hidden until now. John wrote the book of Revelation in the Bible which contains a series of revelations. The revelation I am showing you is related to what is happening and will soon happen on the earth and it involves you," said Alex.

It was then that Dan realized they were back on the mountain top. "Wow, this was not a dream before, or was it?"

"Now, tell me what you have learned so far," said Alex. "What does all of this represent?"

Dan wanted to make a big impression so he began enthusiastically, "It all has to do with all the things that are happening on the earth today. There were terrorist bombings in London and Miami today. These types of things have to do with the earthquakes and the things falling down. There are also all kinds of natural disasters that have to do with the big hurricane like storm and things being moved around." As Dan watched the expression on Alex's face as he finished the last statement, the air just went out of his sails.

Alex wasn't impressed at all, "Dan! Those are all just surface things. These things you are talking about are only distractions to you right now. They have their place, but they are not the things you need to focus on. You have to look deeper, underneath the surface."

"What do you mean? I don't understand," said Dan. Even the sails were starting to fall now. Instead of impressing Alex, he showed how little he did know.

"Do you remember when I was talking to you about the spiritual world?" asked Alex.

"Sure, I remember," replied Dan.

"Things happen in the spiritual realm too," began Alex. "Do you remember the words of the Lord when He was here on the earth? He spoke the words and they became a reality. Reality does not just happen. He said, 'If you have faith the size of a mustard seed, you can say to this mountain, be removed and be cast into the sea and it will obey.'

It does not take a large amount faith, but it does take the spoken word. The spoken word on earth changes a lot of things. It is the seed and it makes things happen in the spiritual realm, both good and bad. Can you see the connection?"

"I think so," replied Dan. "It's like earlier with the encounter with that demon, when I called out for help, you came."

"That is right," said Alex, "and that is only a small example of the power of the spoken word and the authority behind it."

"Now," Alex continued, "let's get back to the vision. Every person has a purpose, talent and a God-given destiny. Whether they walk it out depends on them and the choices they make with their lives. Each person is only responsible for what has been given to them. However, their own selfish desires can affect the outcome of their destiny."

"So, what are all these rocks that keep falling and getting pushed and blown around?" asked Dan. This had been bothering him from the very beginning.

"The rocks are people's dreams. Some of the dreams are God-given, some are the dreams of others for that individual, and some of them are just the individual's personal dreams and desires," replied Alex. "Before we go on with this, let's go back to the beginning where you saw all of the individual islands and other structures that were sticking out of the water."

"Yes, what were those?" asked Dan eagerly. Finally, he was going to get some answers. "They all looked like ancient ruins."

"Well, in a sense, they are," said Alex. "However, that is not all they are. Each ghost-like structure represented a kingdom that had ruled on the earth for a period of time, but is now just a memory of the past. However, some of the islands represent a particular revelation and move of God. You see, over the centuries God has been restoring truth back to His Bride, the Church. It all starts with someone who gets a revelation, similar to what is happening with you right now."

"Wow!" exclaimed Dan as he got excited. "Would that be people like Martin Luther and John Wesley?"

"Yes, it would," Alex continued.

"But why are they just islands in the past?" asked Dan. This did not make any sense to him.

"Each of these islands is like a memorial," Alex began again. "The church is being built upon the foundation of the revelation of Jesus Christ. He is the cornerstone. The foundation is laid by the apostles and prophets. Upon this foundation new revelations must be added. Anything that is added that is not truth will weaken the structure that is being built. This is where the storms and earthquakes have their place. Everything will be shaken at various times. Nothing will remain that is not built according to the Master's plan."

"So how does this massive structure fit into the picture?" asked Dan.

"There are many who are building on a foundation," replied Alex. "Some are building upon the right foundation and their hearts are right. Others are building with some of the borrowed truths of this first group but they are building for their own selfish gain. These are the ones you see with a shallow foundation. Then there is a third group that has camped on a truth from the past and is trying to build, but there isn't any new material to add to the walls. There is also a fourth group beyond this massive structure that you haven't seen yet, they are simply building on an illusion."

"But what does this all mean?" asked Dan. He was hoping that Alex would not mind the interruption again. "How do I fit into this?"

"You are being entrusted with a truth you must proclaim to those who will hear and to those who choose not to hear," continued Alex. "Some will welcome you with open arms, while others will see you as an enemy to the fulfillment of their dreams. They will seek you out to try and destroy you and your reputation. Rest assured, your enemies are as real as the one you saw earlier and they also walk around in flesh and bone."

"But, I am only one person," stated Dan. "How will …"

"... you ever succeed?" finished Alex. "Only by the grace of God and with His help! You will finish just like the others who have gone on before you."

"Like Martin Luther and John Wesley?" asked Dan.

"You are starting to understand," said Alex.

"But some were killed! Will that happen to me?" asked Dan with rather large eyes.

"That isn't for me to say," replied Alex. "Just know that your name is written in the Book of Life and your reward will be waiting for you at the end of your life."

"So what do I need to do now?" asked Dan.

"For now, you need to understand the revelation and share it with those as you are told," replied Alex. "Now, look again at the vision and tell me what you see."

"I see people trying to build individual structures on the massive rock," Dan began. "Some of them are building to protect themselves from the other builders. Some of the structures are barely big enough to protect one person. The people who stay in these are all alone. There are also a lot of people walking around aimlessly. They have no sense of belonging and no place of protection. Over on one side, I see groups of structures with people shooting at each other. As soon as one gets something built up, someone else comes along and tears it down. There are many casualties. On the other side, I see people going back and forth communicating with each other. It looks like they are building a huge structure, however, it seems invisible to most of the people on this rock. This structure is powerful and strong, but it isn't built by the hands of the people within. It looks like each stone has a unique shape and a particular place and each is being put in place by the Lord himself. This structure is not very large at present, but it is very beautiful and strong. In fact, some of these workers are being ridiculed by the other builders of the other structures."

"Now, you are seeing correctly!" exclaimed Alex with some excitement. "Do you know what all of this means?"

"I am not for sure," Dan replied, "but I would really like to know."

"Everyone on top of this rock area believes they are doing the work of the Lord," Alex started. "However, as you can see, this is not true. The easiest way to see this is to focus on the structure the Lord, Himself is building. Now as you pointed out, most of the other builders and people don't even notice what He is doing. Why is that?"

"Well, it looks like they are all caught up with their own projects," replied Dan. He was excited that he was starting to understand the vision. "But, how is it that they are all upon the same rock?"

"That is a good question," said Alex. "Let's go down and take a look at the foundation." Alex took

Dan over to another vantage point where they could get a glimpse at the underside of the structure. "What do you see now?"

"I can see it now. Wow! That is interesting," Dan began. "There is solid rock under the whole structure that the Lord is building. The rock continues deep into the water to the ocean floor. The rock under all the other structures is like a ledge that extends out from the Lord's structure. It is thicker in some places and thinner in others. There are some cracks here and there in the ledge. It is definitely not a sure foundation. Why is that?"

"That part of the ledge foundation has been tainted with other things. This foundation is mixed with pride, selfish ambition, unforgiveness, and other fleshly desires," said Alex. "This ledge will eventually crumble and fall into the sea along with everything attached to it. The time has come for me to leave now. We will meet again soon. You will do well to meditate and pray about what you have seen and heard. Ask the Lord to give you insight. Also, discuss these things with Susan. She has been given a gift that can help as you both continue to walk together. Be careful though, the enemy seeks to sidetrack you so stay alert."

"Thanks Alex," Dan said as the vision slowly faded away. Dan was staring at the ceiling as the morning rays of the sun were coming through his window. He didn't get much sleep this night either, but he felt totally rested. *'What a way to begin a new day,'* he thought. He had just enough time to get ready, eat and get to the office. He went through the motions of getting ready and even as he was driving to work his mind was on the vision he had seen. *'What an exciting time to be alive!'* he thought as he drove up to his parking space. *'I can't wait to share all of this with Susan!'*

Chapter 5

Not Everyone Listens

Dan could hardly wait to talk to Susan, however, as he got out of his car, he began to have doubts about this relationship. *'What if she doesn't believe all of this? I don't know if she could handle the pressure. She seems so delicate,'* he thought. *'I sure hope I am wrong.'* He really hoped this relationship was going to work, but it would be nice to have some reassurance.

Susan saw him first as he walked into his office. She hurriedly went over and walked in, "And how are you this morning?" she asked. She had noticed that he seemed really deep in thought and was wondering what was happening in that head of his. Without waiting for him to reply, she added, "So?"

"So, what?" asked Dan, with a playful grin on his face.

"What do you mean, so what? You know what I'm talking about. Don't you act so innocent, I know you are just messing with me," she added.

"Okay," he said, giving in to her. "It was the most terrifying and most wondrous night, all in one!" Dan knew that this would get her total attention.

"All right, mister," she said, playing along. "Spill it, buster! I want to know everything."

"Well," he began, "I can, but we might not get much work done since this will take a while."

"Don't you do me like that," she grinned. "At least let me know a little bit. What did Alex say about your theory?"

"Oh, that!" replied Dan. "That didn't fly at all. It was way off base. In fact, it totally crashed and burned. The vision means something completely different."

"What did you mean about it being terrifying?" asked Susan in a concerned tone. "What was that all about?"

"Are you sure you want to know?" asked Dan, hesitantly. He was unsure if he should tell her. He didn't want to scare her away.

"I'm not that easy to scare," she replied. "I have had my share of situations and I'm still here, aren't I?" She gave him a playful jab with that last statement.

"Okay, just don't tell me I didn't warn you," he said as he began his story. He had just told her about the demon when she interrupted.

"Oh, it's him again," she interrupted. "Don't pay any attention to him. He just wants to keep you from speaking out and exposing his works," she added so matter-of-factly that it completely amazed Dan.

"Wow, and here I was all concerned about telling

you about this," he added. "So, how is it that you know all about this creature?"

"I was doing some volunteer work a while back and this thing appeared to me also. Of course, I was not where I am right now. It really frightened me then," she replied. "In fact, it almost shipwrecked the work I was doing until someone helped me through it. My faith was really shaken at the time. The spiritual realm is real and when you experience something like that, it makes a lasting impression."

"Tell me about it," said Dan. "It shook me so bad that all I could do was cry out for help. I am so glad Alex was nearby. I don't know what would have happened next. The whole atmosphere had changed. It is hard to explain, but it was so real and powerful."

"Believe me, I know the feeling," she replied, remembering all too well that particular night. "So, what happened next?"

Dan filled her in on the understanding of the vision. He kept watching her in amazement as she seemed to take everything in stride. He was starting to get excited. He remembered what Alex had told him about her gift. His faith was starting to build and he was feeling more at ease.

As Dan was about to continue, Scott, from the art department knocked on his door. "Dan, when you get a moment, can you stop by and look at the new story boards?"

"Sure, I will be there in a few minutes," he replied.

"Okay, thanks," Scott said and then continued on his way.

"I guess this means we will have to pick up later where we left off," said Susan a little annoyed that they were going to have to stop for now.

"I will stop by and talk to you as soon as I take care of this," Dan said. "We really need to get this project to the multimedia department so they can get cranking on it. The client has wanted so many changes that this project is getting behind schedule."

"See you in a little while," she said with a smile. She went back to her office, sat down at her desk and stared at the computer monitor on her desk. The more she was around Dan, the more she wanted to be around him. He was not like a lot of other guys she knew. He was real and sensitive. She hoped that he felt the same about her. She was hoping that her past relationships would not affect this relationship. She was fighting through all of the fears that seemed to keep popping up here and there. She was most vulnerable to them at night when she was all alone. When she was with Dan, however, the fears seemed to be non-existent and unfounded. She wanted to bring it up to Dan, but it seemed so trivial, plus there just didn't seem to be enough time and she didn't want to spoil a good thing.

Dan was busy with projects the rest of the day, so

he didn't get a chance to talk to Susan until around four o'clock. "Hi!" he said, as he stuck his head through the doorway.

Susan jerked her head up quickly. Dan's sudden appearance had startled her and her heart was racing. "Wow that scared me! Where have you been all day?"

"Oh, just trying to get caught up with that project. We are going to have to get an outside agency to help us with some of the work. It is more detailed and time consuming than we thought," he began. "If we get any more projects like this, I am going to have to hire more people. Some of these agencies just don't understand what we need. They have their own ways of doing things and they aren't listening to our needs."

"Well, just let me know and I will get the word out," Susan said. "Hey, do you want to go with me over to Kathy's Hangout this evening?"

"Sure, that sounds great," said Dan. "How about I bring my laptop and we can play a game or something?"

"Okay," said Susan. "I will pick you up at six o'clock sharp."

"Don't be late," he chided. "I will be expecting you."

Susan was sitting in front of the mirror and

putting on her makeup when a memory came into her thoughts. It was the night of her first date and she was so nervous that night. She had spent a lot of time making sure everything was perfect. She had the feeling of butterflies inside. The same thing was happening tonight, except for the fact that she was wearing jeans and a nice pullover sweater. *'It is amazing what can happen in a couple of days. What a difference a few days can make in someone's life,'* she thought. *"Lord, thank you for watching over me and taking care of me. I was really beginning to wonder if anything exciting was going to happen with me again. Now, I see why you wanted me to take this job. I wouldn't have met Dan if I would have gone with that other company, even though it looked like the better deal. You are so wonderful. You are worthy of my praise. I love You. Help me have a great evening with Dan and help me be the person You want me to be. He is so special. Thank You for bringing him into my life."*

She looked up at the clock and quickly got up to grab everything as she walked towards the door. Above her doorway was a sign that read, *'Let your light shine into the darkness so that the lost might find their way.'*

Dan was already walking out of the door as Susan parked at the curb. He noticed her eyes beaming with happiness as their eyes met. He held her gaze for a moment and let her life touch his. She was so beautiful. It was then he noticed the glow around her face. "What happened to you?" he asked. She looked like she had heard the most wonderful story in her life.

"Oh, I'm sorry," she replied. "I just got all caught up thinking about you and talking to the Lord. Everything is just marvelous. I just want to enjoy this moment." She leaned over as he sat down and kissed him on the cheek.

Dan took the kiss in stride. "Wow, it must have been a good conversation for me to get a kiss. So, just what were you talking about?"

"Oh, I was just telling Him how much I appreciate Him and love Him. I also told Him how happy I am that He put us together and how I was glad not to have taken that other job," she said.

"Yeah, I'm glad you didn't take that other job either," he added. "I would have missed out all the way around."

"Ready to go?" she asked as she put the car in gear.

They walked into Kathy's Hangout a little while later and sat down at a table near the window. As they were sitting down, Sheri and Joan came over to the table from the other side of the room. "Hi, Susan," said Sheri. "Who is this?" she added with a grin.

Susan had already told them both about her and

Dan. They were both excited for her. She had been through some tough times and they were glad that things were changing for her.

Susan introduced them to Dan and they all sat down together. A short while later, Jennifer, a friend of Joan's came by and joined them. They talked for a while about the latest events in the news and the bombings. After a while, the conversation started to get a little heated. The discussion had turned to prophetic dreams and visions. As Dan began talking about his vision, at Susan's request, Jennifer was getting noticeably more uncomfortable. Finally, she spoke out, "I don't believe in visions. I had a vision once and none of it came true. In fact, everything went the opposite way and it was really tragic. It wrecked people's lives. I need to go now. I will see you later Joan."

"Okay, Jennifer," replied Joan. "Are you going to be all right?"

"Yeah, sure! I just need to get away and calm down," said Jennifer. She was visibly shaking all over. All of a sudden the events of the past began to play out in her thoughts.

As Jennifer walked out of the door, Susan said, "Joan, I think you need to go with her. She doesn't need to go through this alone."

"I was thinking the same thing," Joan replied. "I will see you guys later. It was good meeting you, Dan. I would like to hear the rest some other time if that is okay with you?"

"Sure," said Dan. "Give us a call if you need to. In the meantime we will pray for you and Jennifer. Tell her I'm sorry if I hurt her. I didn't mean to."

"You didn't say anything wrong," said Joan. "It just brought up some old memories that have been haunting her. Pray for healing and comfort and that I will be able to speak the right words to her. See you guys later."

"I'll go with you," said Sheri as she grabbed her things. She could feel that Joan was going to need some help.

After Joan and Sheri had left, Dan continued, "I am sorry. I didn't mean for anyone to get hurt."

"It wasn't your fault," Susan began. "Not everyone will be able to or want to hear. For Jennifer, this will be a time of healing if she will receive it. Some people really don't want to be healed. To them, their pain becomes a crutch and an excuse to not go on with life. They get caught up in self pity. Let's pray that Jennifer can hear the truth and receive the healing that is available to her." Dan joined Susan in prayer as they prayed for her healing. They prayed that she would receive her healing and comfort from the Lord.

"Maybe I just need to be more careful about who I share this with," said Dan. "I don't like seeing people get hurt. Maybe I shouldn't share it with anyone else."

"That would be foolish. You have to share it with whomever the Lord tells you to, regardless of what anyone else thinks. Whether they choose to receive or reject it is up to them," Susan said with a sense of urgency.

"You know, that is the same thing Alex told me during the vision. I had forgotten about that until now," said Dan. "I just don't like to see people hurting."

"Neither do I," Susan began. "But it will happen more and more as you share this vision with others. In fact, some will get really angry at you and it will not be your fault. You can't stop. Everyone has to make their own choices. You will be held responsible if you don't share."

"What a responsibility," said Dan. "I didn't sign up for this."

"It is your love, compassion and understanding that will help others to hear the truth and maybe dare to hear how it applies to their lives. They need to allow the truth to change their lives and set them free. If they don't, they will continue to walk around all wounded and torn," said Susan. She was really beginning to see the depth of love for others in Dan. He was a very special person and she felt honored to be his friend.

Chapter 6

The Next Horizon

That night was uneventful for a change and finally the weekend arrived. He awoke in the morning having not remembered if he even had a dream during the night. In fact, the whole day came and went without any major challenges. His brother had called during the day and invited him to Bar-B-Q for lunch tomorrow at his house. Dan accepted and asked if he could bring a guest. He stopped by Susan's office and invited her to go with him which she gladly accepted. Susan had a meeting to go to that evening so they agreed for Dan to pick her up the next morning.

"How was your meeting?" asked Dan as Susan met him curb side.

"Oh, it went great," she replied. "I would rather have been with you, though."

"Oh, really?" Dan questioned sarcastically.

"Yes, you are really starting to grow on me, I guess," Susan remarked in response to the sarcasm.

Susan brought Dan up to date on the Advertising

Seminar she attended while they were driving over to his brother's house. John and his wife Nikki lived a short distance out of the city up in the hills. It was really beautiful this time of year with the trees changing the color of their leaves. The first cool front of the season had blown through last night, so the air was a little nippy. It was a really nice day. The sun was shining and it was going to be good to be with his brother again.

The door to the house opened as they drove up into the driveway. John came out to meet them as they got out of the car. Dan gave his older brother a big hug. "It is so good to see you, John. I have been looking forward to this all week."

"Wow! Now, that is a welcome! What have I done to receive this kind of greeting?" asked John quizzically.

"Well, originally there was only one reason I was eagerly waiting to see you, but as the week went on another one presented itself. John, I would like you to meet my special friend and co-worker, Susan," said Dan.

"It is good to meet you, Susan," said John as they hugged each other. "You must be very special for Dan to be this excited."

"It is good to meet you too, John," Susan returned. "Dan has told me a lot about you."

"I hope it has all been good," said John jokingly. "So, what was the other reason, Dan?"

Dan started to fill John in about the vision as they gathered their things out of the car and went inside. Nikki met them in the foyer as they entered the house. "Hi, Dan," she said as she gave him a hug. "And who is this with you?" she asked as she gently nudged him.

Dan replied with a grin on his face, "This is my dear friend, Susan. I thought I would bring someone better looking than myself so you all would not get bored looking at me all the time."

Nikki laughed, "Yeah, right! Hi, Susan! It is so good to meet you. It looks like you two are a little closer than friends though," she interjected as they hugged each other.

Susan grinned, "Is it that easy to see?"

"I know Dan pretty well and I know when he is serious. I am so glad for you both," said Nikki. "Here, let me have your jackets and I will hang them up for you. Come on in to the living room. The food is almost ready."

Soon the food was ready and they all moved into the dining room. "Okay, Dan, why don't you tell us about your vision," suggested John. "If you don't mind starting at the beginning again for Nikki's sake, that would be great."

Dan started again at the beginning of the vision and filled in everything including getting together with Susan and all the current events. "That is very interesting," John added after Dan had finished.

"You know what this means, don't you Dan?"

"I think I am starting to see the broader picture, but feel free to fill me in on what you see," replied Dan. "My life is changing very rapidly at this point. I have to watch what I say and who I say it to. People are starting to take things personally."

"I think you are getting the major points. Nikki and I will help and support you as much as we can. I think the major part of our help will be in prayer, though," said John. "Both of you will need to stay focused. There will be many opportunities to get sidetracked on issues and things that don't really matter. How is your business doing?"

"It is starting to really come together now. We may need to hire more people here in the future, especially if we get some more contracts," replied Dan.

"You might also start looking for someone to take your place, at least part-time," added John. "Believe me, you will be doing some traveling soon."

"What do you mean?" asked Dan curiously.

"This vision and the way it is unfolding, means you will be sent to meet and talk to others here in America and probably around the world," John watched his brother's eyes as he spoke. "Have you given any thought to this?"

"No, I haven't. This is all really new to me," said Dan. "I think I have come a long way though, considering it all started on Tuesday. I guess we'll just have to take everything one step at a time. What do you make of this?"

"One thing I would suggest," interjected Nikki, "is to write the vision down and any thing else that you think might be relevant to it including current news and events. This way you will have a record of everything and will not have to rely on your memory. Sometimes our memories can change when experience adds to the equation."

"I agree," said John. "That is good advice. Susan, where do you fit into this?"

"I am not totally sure yet," she replied. She had not expected this question. "I have been honored to help Dan in any way that I can. I feel that I can help support him in this. I've had some experience in this area and I know I would like to be with him."

John began, "One thing is for sure, you are not going to be the most admired couple around. There is a minority that will welcome you and pray for you because you represent the truth. Those who oppose you the most will be those who are religious. Some will gather around you because you speak the truth, while others will want to be near you because of your popularity. Dan, do you remember when Nikki and I first started out in ministry?"

"Yeah, I do," began Dan. "At the time I thought you had lost your mind. But if you had not stood up for what you believed, I would not have even known the Lord. I am so grateful to you both. I have watched your lives and that encourages me even now with what is happening to us. I will be leaning on you both for a lot of advice."

Nikki began, "Susan, will you come with me into the study. I would like to show you something?"

"Sure," replied Susan. She was beaming with excitement and was feeling totally accepted by Nikki and John. "I would love to."

"We'll be back shortly," said Nikki as they started to leave the room.

After they had left the room, Dan turned to John. "So, what do you think about Susan?"

"I think you had better watch out," John teased. "Just kidding, but seriously, I really like her. You really need someone who can help you walk this out and I believe she is just the one to do it. She looks like she has been through some things herself and has had to stand her ground. I don't think she will be one to give up quickly when things take a turn every now and then."

"How did you see all of that?" asked Dan. He proceeded to give him a little background on Susan. He told him about the volunteer organization that she had worked for. "When I told her about the dream she just jumped right in to help me. There wasn't any fear at all. I have never been around anyone like her with the exception of Nikki."

"Yeah, I agree," said John. "Nikki is a special

lady and so is Susan. The Lord knows how to put us together with those who complement us. Believe me, the feeling is mutual. There are many things that try to tear us apart and it is good to have someone with you who doesn't have selfish motives. The focus has to be on His Kingdom and not on ours. The only building that will stand in these times is the one He is building."

"That is very interesting you said that," Dan said. "That was the main focus of the vision I was starting to tell you about. If you know about that, then why has the Lord told me that I need to share this with others? How many people already know this stuff?"

"It is not about how many people know or don't know. It is about you being obedient to fulfilling your destiny. You have been anointed to reach a certain group of people. Whether or not they listen is not up to you," said John. "Those who are truly seeking the truth will find it. Those who are seeking their own way will find that, too. It just will not end the way they think it will. There is a scripture I would like to share with you. I am going to put it in my own words and I would like for you to tell me what it means to you. The Lord said, 'Many will come to Me in that day and say to Me, "Lord, look at all we have done in Your Name. We have healed the sick, cast out demons and done all of these things."' Then He replies, 'Away from Me you evil doers. I never knew you.'"

"Wow, that is heavy," replied Dan. "I'm not sure what that means. How is it they can do all of those things without Him knowing them? That doesn't seem possible."

"That is what I thought at first," John began, "but as I began to meditate on it, I realized that these people just used the scriptures for their own gain and agendas. They never developed their own relationship with Him. Let me give you an example. Say for instance, there is a rich man. He marries a lovely bride and they build this house together and they start to build their family. She has the rights to everything of his. She has his name so therefore, she can do pretty much anything she wants. Something happens and she decides that she is not getting enough attention. All of the attention is going to him. So she starts doing things for herself and uses his name to do it. She stops letting him into her heart and starts pushing him away. She even starts her own business and accomplishes a lot of things, but they live on separate sides of the house. She eventually starts seeing someone else. What do you think the end result of this relationship will be?"

"He will divorce her, of course," replied Dan.

"Exactly!" stated John. "That is what the Lord is saying in this verse. There are many who are using His name to build their own kingdoms. They are gathering His people to themselves. Not only are they not having a relationship with Him, but they are keeping others from Him. This is a very dangerous place to be."

"You have just explained some more of the vision," said Dan excitedly. "Why didn't He give you this vision?"

"It isn't for me, Dan," replied John. "It isn't for me to choose. However, I will help you in any way I can."

"Well, how do I do this?" asked Dan.

"You do as He tells you," said John. "If He is not telling you to do anything, then rest."

"But I don't know enough about all of this," said Dan seriously.

"And you never will," replied John quickly. "Sometimes it is easier to hear Him when you don't know much. It is then you are teachable. Some people know so much they have become unteachable and no longer make a difference. You must become like a child. You must believe Him like a child believes in their parents, always trusting them for everything."

Nikki had just finished sharing their wedding photos with Susan when she decided it was time to ask her a question. "So what do you think about you and Dan?"

"I was wondering when that question was going

to be asked," Susan began. "I am not sure yet. I know that I am excited and this week has been totally wonderful, but it has only been a very short time. Up until this week, I have only known Dan at work. I haven't had a relationship like this before. It is like something you only dream about. What can I say, but I would like it to never end. I feel totally caught up in this and it is just great."

"I thought so," Nikki began. "That is similar to the way John and I met. I met John just before he got out of seminary. We both went to the same church. He was really on fire. It seemed like there wasn't anything he couldn't do. A short while later he met up with some serious opposition. Most of his friends stopped talking to him and the church decided to ask him to leave. He was devastated."

"What did he do?" asked Susan. "He looks all right now."

"It was during that time we got together," Nikki replied. "I saw what happened and it was not John's fault. He too had received a vision from the Lord about some of the things that were going on with certain individuals in the church and decided to share it with the elders. Unfortunately, they decided not to listen and furthermore they all stood up against him and told him to leave."

"That must have been horrible!" exclaimed Susan. She was shocked. "What did he do?"

"For a while he was thinking about leaving the

ministry all together," said Nikki. "That was when we were in one of those, 'right time at the right place' moments. He needed to talk to someone who would not judge him and I happened to be the one. Of course, now we know it wasn't by coincidence. We made it through one day at a time. Dan has seen some of what was going on and it was through those times that he came to know the Lord in a deeper way for himself. So, all in all, a lot of good things came out of that situation."

"What happened to that church and the elders?" asked Susan.

"It was only a short time later that the vision came to pass and they all separated and the church is gone now," said Nikki. "There were a lot of people who got hurt in the process. John and I eventually got married and we just continue to walk one day at a time. It is always an adventure. There have been some ups and downs, but I would not trade it for the world. We have been able to help some of the people get healed. We have a group of people we meet with weekly now and who knows where it will lead. We have people calling us from all over the world now who have heard our story."

"That is great!" exclaimed Susan. "What a turnaround. I like the way God works."

"I do too. I can't think of a better way to live," said Nikki. "Let's go and check on the guys and see what they are up to. They are probably talking about you."

"So, what have you two been talking about all this time?" asked Nikki, as they walked into the room. "It was not about us, was it?"

"No, actually we were talking about children," piped John. He wanted to see what kind of a response he would get from this one.

"Children?" asked Susan, being caught off guard. "Ah, don't you think you are putting the cart before the horse, mister?" She was amused and her eyes were aimed directly to Dan.

"Oh, it isn't what you think," replied Dan apologetically. "John was just talking about trusting the Lord like a child."

"All right," said Nikki, "I guess we will let it slide then." At that comment they all started laughing. Nikki could not remember them having so much fun together. She was really thankful to have a new friend.

They talked together for a while, mostly just getting to know each other more. Susan felt totally welcomed into this new family. Things were finally working out for her. The loneliness was distancing itself from her. Later, after she had gotten home and settled in, she started thinking about everything that had happened during the week. Her life seemed totally out of control, and yet it was under a control that she felt very familiar with. *"Thank You, Lord, for guiding my life."* That night, she slept better than she could ever remember. She awoke early in the morning feeling totally refreshed. She was really enjoying this new life. *"I think I could get used to this,"* she thought to herself.

Dan had an enjoyable time to himself that evening also. He felt like he was on top of a mountain. It felt like that for the first time in his life, he was doing what he was created to do. He even thought about what it would be like to be married. Susan was such a wonderful person. He too, thanked the Lord. He also had a good night's rest.

John and Nikki stayed up late talking to each other. They were so happy for the new couple and at the same time they were concerned. They knew how things could change in an instant and determined they would make themselves available to Dan and Susan, to help them any way they could. They prayed together before they went to sleep.

Chapter 7

Climbing Higher

The next day, Dan picked Susan up around two o'clock in the afternoon and they went over to John's ministry center. John said that he had special guests coming in from different parts of the world and he wanted Dan and Susan to meet them.

As Dan and Susan entered the building they saw John at the back. "Dan," said John, "last night after you and Susan left, I felt like I needed to ask you to share your vision with the group. When I talked to Nikki about it this morning, she said she had a dream and in it you were sharing your vision at today's meeting. So, it is official. How do you feel about it?"

"I guess that is okay with me," said Dan. "What all do you want me to share?"

"Just whatever comes to your mind," replied John. "There are some leaders here today who need to hear what you have to say. Their lives will be changed. They have been asking the Lord what they need to be sharing with their people and I think this word will help them understand what is happening in their communities."

Dan shared his vision with the group and afterwards he met with some of the people. They each had their own questions for him. They were particularly interested in the Lord's structure and the people who were helping Him build. He also received eight invitations to come over to their meetings to share the vision. This would take him around the world. Things were changing rapidly. He felt like he had been strapped to a rocket and it had just lifted off. If everything went according to the requests, he was going to be busy every weekend for the next two or three months.

Later on, Dan, Susan, John and Nikki went over to the El Serena Café. Susan filled them in on the place as they drove over.

"This is wonderful," exclaimed Nikki, as they walked out to the back of the café. What a nice way to close out a wonderful weekend."

John looked over at Dan and Susan and he couldn't remember a time when his brother looked so happy. He just hoped that this journey would not be too dangerous. People liked their places of comfort, power and influence. This generation indulges in entertainment and comfort. They have a tendency to lash out at those who might threaten their style of living. "What are your plans?" John asked Dan.

"I don't know yet," replied Dan. "All of this has taken me by surprise. If we are to travel a lot, I will have to have someone who can oversee the business. It will have to be someone I can trust."

"What about Tim," asked Susan? "He knows the business really well and he has been with you from the beginning."

"That is exactly who I was thinking about. I will talk to him tomorrow and I will also see if Marsha can fill in for you," said Dan.

"Looks like you have everything taken care of then, at least for the time being," said John.

"Almost," Dan began. "I would like for you and Nikki to fly with us when we go to these other places. We can take my corporate jet. I think it would be safer if we were all together and not flying in the commercial airlines. It is a whole different situation when you journey into a foreign country. There are many dangers lurking in the shadows, if you know what I mean."

"You are right," said Susan. "Even Jesus sent His disciples out two by two. We have to be on our guard at all times. When I was doing that volunteer work in Guatemala, we always had to have someone else with us. It wasn't safe to go out alone."

"I think that would be great," Nikki said all excited. "I think I could get used to traveling. What do you say, John?"

"That does sound wonderful, however, I need to

make sure I have someone in place to fill in for the ministry. We also need to make sure the Lord wants us to do this. Just because it seems good, doesn't make it the right thing to do," John replied.

"Why don't we get together next Saturday and share what we have heard through the week? I will see if we can get the business in order and you see if you can work everything out with your ministry," said Dan.

John replied, "That sounds good. Well, Nikki, are you ready to start to packing?"

"Already started," she replied teasingly. "Where are we off to first?"

"Bob Fischer would like me to speak at his conference on the 17th, which is only three weeks away," said Dan. "They will be meeting in Sydney. He will be sending me all the details as soon as he gets back. He is expecting around 200 plus people from the southeastern area of Australia."

"Have you thought about using the internet?" asked John.

"No, I haven't," said Dan.

"That would be a good way to update everyone as you receive more on the vision," said Nikki.

"We definitely have the team that can create and get the site up and running quickly," said Susan enthusiastically. "I can do some sketches when I get home tonight to get things going."

"We'll call a special meeting in the morning

and get everyone together so we can get this going. John, I would like you and Nikki to be there also. We could use your input," said Dan.

"Sure, what time are you thinking?" John asked. "I have a short meeting at eight o'clock, but I should be able to make it by ten. Will that work?"

"That should be fine," said Dan. "That will give me time to bring Tim and Marsha up to speed on all of the developments."

"It sounds like we have a plan then," said Susan.

"Sure does," said John. "Well, I guess we should be going, seeing how busy we will be tomorrow. I would like to spend some time meditating on what we have discussed and make sure we are heading in the right direction."

That night, Alex met with Dan again. "Dan, I have been sent to give you a warning. When you get to Sydney, you need to be cautious. Bob is going to be sharing parts of what he has heard of your vision with his team when he gets back, but there is someone on his team who has been trying to discredit him. This person has been waiting for the right opportunity and will be trying to use this conference to do it. He has been given time to repent and has chosen not to, so he will be exposed at the meeting. After the meeting, he will use parts of the vision to try and turn others against you, Bob, and the Lord's purpose. You need to share this with Susan, Bob, John and Nikki so you can lift this up in prayer and be alert."

Dan could hardly believe his ears, "What are you trying to tell me, Alex? How can I deal with all of this?"

"This is a war," Alex started. "All of this began in the spiritual realm. The enemy knows that if you succeed, his kingdom will suffer a great blow. Believe me, he will do all he can to stop you."

"How can I win then? I can't even see him. He is invisible!" Dan added.

"Only by walking close to the Lord," said Alex. "The Lord has provided you with good counsel. Listen to them and let every plan be established by at least two witnesses. Your safety and success depends on it. I have to go for now."

Dan awoke out of his sleep and noticed that it was time for him to get up. As he was preparing for the day he pondered all that Alex had spoken to him. Fear was knocking on his door again. *"How am I going to do all of this?"* he questioned. *"How can I keep Susan safe?"*

As quickly as those thoughts had passed, he heard a small still voice, *'I Am!'* Suddenly, he felt a wonderful peace envelope his whole being and he knew that everything was going to be all right.

Chapter 8

Many Are The Plans Of A Man

As soon as Dan arrived at work, he met with Susan, Tim and Marsha. He filled them in on the new changes he wanted to implement immediately. Then he had them contact everyone else to meet in the conference room at ten o'clock. While Tim and Marsha were busy getting ready for the meeting, he brought Susan up to speed on the meeting with Alex. She was really concerned and she agreed with him that he needed to get in touch with Bob as soon as possible.

"Will you call Bob and see if we can get a conference call scheduled for noon?" he asked Susan. "I would like John and Nikki to join us on the call, since they will be here. While you are doing that, I will call Sam at the airport and let him know the details of the flight so he can get everything set up. They have been doing some scheduled maintenance on the plane so I want to be sure that everything is ready for us. I want to make sure we have taken care of every detail that is in our power to do."

"Dan!" she said quietly. "Peace to you," she added as she put her hand on his shoulder. "Remember, don't get all stressed out about this. The Lord is fully aware of everything that is happening and if we follow His direction it will all work out and in His timing."

"Thanks," he said as he put his hand on hers, "for helping me to focus. When you said 'peace' I remembered this morning when I heard the Lord speak. He just simply whispered, 'I Am,' and then this peace just flooded over me. That is exactly what is happening now."

"Great! I will go and make that call," said Susan as she started walking to the door.

Dan sat back in his chair and relaxed for a moment. He was used to handling a lot of information at a time and delegating it out to those who needed it, but this was a whole new realm he was walking in. He would have to remember to take some time out before making split decisions. He was not in charge anymore. He had given up that right for the Lord's purpose and plan for his life. He knew that he had made the right decision. His life had already changed for the better and he wouldn't trade this for anything else.

The meeting went really well with his people. He introduced John and Nikki to the group. He also let them know about the changes with Tim, Marsha, and Susan. Everyone seemed to be excited about the new changes and was eager to begin their new assignments. Susan shared her new layouts for the new web site. Marsha was put in charge of developing the story boards with her department. Tim is going to give Scott some of his duties. Hopefully, the new site will be up and operational by the time they get back from Australia.

After the meeting, John, Susan and Nikki joined Dan back in his office. "What a crew!" exclaimed John. "The Lord has really blessed you with a wonderful group of people. Be ready for this business to explode. I believe that once you get the new site up and operational with all the new technology in place, there are going to be a lot of others out there who will want something similar."

"No problem!" replied Dan with a smile. "We will just add it to everything else that is going on."

"Have you thought about incorporating your new assignment into the business?" asked Nikki.

"Yes I have," replied Dan. "I am so glad you mentioned that. I wasn't going to say anything until someone else brought it up first. I am thinking about letting the business help support the expenses of the ministry. That way, everything that we share can go out freely to those who want the information."

"What will you do about printing costs," asked Susan, "especially when you start printing booklets and books?"

"We will handle what we can. Most of the

material will be published to the web site. I am thinking that for those who want the printed material, at some point we might have to charge for printing, shipping and handling. My main focus will be to share the information as best as I can so that everyone can hear." said Dan. "I am open to any ideas on this matter."

"That sounds great," said John. "There are so many leaders who produce a lot of materials just to increase their wealth and have forgotten the main purpose of their calling and who the message was intended for in the first place. So many parts of the church have literally become a marketplace."

"I have also been thinking about other things we can do," Dan began, "but I am not sure the Lord is in them. I think we have enough time to make sure what He wants us to do before we implement a new project. There are a lot of people I would like to help."

"I agree," said Susan. "It is so good to hear you say that. I have seen people get used by the Lord in a certain way and the next thing you know they add a bunch of other things to it. Pretty soon they get lost in all the confusion, soon everything collapses and then they get very discouraged and depressed. The whole work gets destroyed."

"We have seen a lot of that also," interjected Nikki. "Sometimes these people get so hurt by all the accusations that are spoken against them that they turn away from the Lord altogether."

"So, what do we need to do to get ready for this trip?" asked Dan. "We have a call in to Bob and are waiting for him to call back. The plane will be ready for the trip. Let's see, it is the beginning of spring there, so it might be a little colder than it is here, so we need to pack accordingly. Bob is going to take care of all the hotel and transportation in Sydney for us."

"That is great," said John. "That trying to get used to driving on the wrong side of the road is hard. Oh, I'm sorry, I mean the left side rather than the right," he added as the play on words amused him.

"Aw, come on," chided Nikki, "it's not that bad. You managed last time didn't you?"

"Yeah, I guess I did," answered John. "It was the sidewalk that was hard to navigate. I forgot to look to the right instead of the left before I tried to cross the intersection. I am glad you were there to warn me. That car was coming really fast."

"Well, someone has to watch out for you," continued Nikki with her playful remarks.

"Yes and I am certainly glad you do," John said as he turned to give her a hug. They loved to have fun with each other and took advantage of it every chance they got.

"This is beginning to sound more like a vacation than a serious trip." Dan piped as he watched John and Nikki having some fun.

"It is going to be a vacation anyway," Susan chimed in. "I have never been to Australia, so just being there will be good for me. Hopefully, we have some extra time to do a little sight seeing. I have always wanted to check out the city."

"You are going to love it," said Nikki as she reflected on the last time she and John were there. "It is absolutely beautiful."

A voice came through the phone. It was Sharon, Dan's receptionist. "Dan, Bob is on line two."

"Thanks, Sharon," Dan said as he pushed the button to put Bob on the speaker. "Hi, Bob! I have John, Nikki and Susan here with me. How are you today or should I say so early in the morning?"

"It is rather early here, but I have been up all night anyway," he replied. "It is going to be good to get some sleep soon. I've had to put out a few fires already. I had a meeting with my people as soon as I got back and it has caused quite a stir. It caught me by surprise. I was so excited after I left your meeting that I spent the whole flight back just thinking about it with the exception of a little nap. Sometimes I forget that not everyone is with me."

"We have most of the arrangements for the trip complete and everything seems to be going great," said John. "How is Cindy?"

"Oh, she is doing great," Bob replied, referring to his lovely wife. "I think I have seen her for about all of twenty minutes, but we have a date planned for tomorrow."

"Bob," Dan began, "there is something I need to share with you." Dan shared with him everything that Alex warned him about.

"Wow!" Bob exclaimed and then he was silent for a moment. "I know that not everyone is close to me, but I can't think of anyone who would do something like that. I am really sorry to hear that. Are you sure you still want to come? I would hate to put you through all of that." He was really saddened by the information that Alex had relayed to Dan.

"That, we have to do," Dan replied. "At least we know what to expect and we will be ready. I am sure glad we have advance warning."

"Me too, mate! Me too!" Bob said, encouraged by the fact they were going to stand with him in this. "I just don't understand. You would think that this stuff wouldn't happen among brothers and sisters. Thanks for the heads up though. Cindy and I will be praying. This just helps to confirm that this message is for now. We need to know who we can trust these days. We have a project I am supposed to be sharing soon with my people, so I am glad this is happening before I do that."

"Why don't you go ahead and get some rest and call me later and we can go over any necessary details," asked Dan.

"That is a good idea," replied Bob. "This day has been long enough. I will talk to you later."

After they had said their good-byes, Dan hung up the phone. "I think I am starting to see some of this warfare Alex was talking about."

"It's really sad when it involves leaders. People are usually forced to choose a side and there is a tearing of hearts," said Nikki. She was really emotional as she felt the actual tearing begin. She reached for a tissue to dry her eyes.

Susan went over to her and gave her a hug. They embraced for a while until Nikki stopped crying. "I'm sorry."

"There is no need to be sorry," said Nikki. "The Lord, Himself weeps at times like these. It is His love that continues to reach out to everyone. He does not want even one to be lost. It is an honor to experience His love for others. It was that compassion that enabled Him to endure the cross with its terrible pain and humiliation."

"Thanks, Nikki," said Dan. "I needed to hear that right now. I was really beginning to get frustrated over the situation in Sydney. Sometimes I think it is too easy to focus on the problem and not the people involved."

"That is for sure, and I know we have all been there," said John. "How can we ever understand at all if we are not willing to share in His suffering? When things were going well for me, I had many friends. It was when things turned that I realized who my friends really were and it was far fewer than I thought. May our eyes be opened to the truth so that we might see clearly."

Chapter 9

The Confrontation

The time had passed by quickly as the group made all the necessary preparations for their trip. Finally, Friday morning had arrived. Dan had picked up Susan and they met John and Nikki at the airport. The morning air felt great and invigorating as they walked the short distance to the hangar. Sam had the plane waiting and ready. They loaded up their luggage, boarded and taxied down the runway. Everything was going smooth.

Dan was thinking how good it was going to be to get away for a while. He had put a lot of hours in to make his business a success. Now he has a lot of capable people who can keep it running smoothly. "Is everyone comfortable?" he asked.

"I am," John replied as he was relaxing in one of the large leather recliners. "Man, this is the way to travel. We need to do this more often."

"I agree," said Nikki. "I like this plane. No waiting in line and no cramped seats."

"If you need anything, make yourselves at home.

We have some food, snacks and drinks at the back," said Dan. "Susan, do you need anything?"

"No thanks, I am fine. I'm just enjoying the moment," she replied. "This is great."

The trip seemed a lot shorter than it really was. Everyone was so excited about visiting with each other and also looking forward to seeing all the sites in Sydney.

After they arrived and walked into the terminal, they met Bob and he took them to the hotel. After they had checked in and freshened up from the trip, they all met down at the restaurant in the hotel. Bob had reserved a large table and there were three couples with him including his wife, Cindy. "It is really good to meet you all," said Cindy after Bob had introduced everyone. "Bob told me about the meeting and the vision. It is going to be interesting to see how it all unfolds."

Even though they lived in a different country, you would have thought they were already good friends. "That is the thing I like about meeting the Lord's people. It is like we already know each other," said John.

They discussed the meeting that would start in the morning. Bob had shared the warning with those he had brought with him. "Dan, do you have any idea who this person is?" he asked.

"No, the only thing I am sure of is that we will know by the end of the meeting," Dan replied.

"I have gone over and over in my mind and I can't think of anyone who would want to do that," Bob added. "I just don't get it. If they are so unhappy, why don't they come and talk to me or just leave? Why do they have to cause such a stir?"

"Unfortunately, that is the way it usually is," replied John visibly saddened. "The enemy is always trying to destroy the Lord's work and it seems like he is always able to find the people who can do the most damage. I'm just glad he warns us in advance and helps us to know what to do. Who knows, maybe this situation can be turned for good before it is all over."

"That would be wonderful," said Cindy. "We will definitely be praying that way. I don't like to see anyone get hurt. This person must have been really hurt to react this way."

"You know, I haven't seen anything more dangerous than a wounded animal," began Bob as he was reflecting on a previous incident, "and how much more so is a person who has been wounded and is feeling cornered."

After they had eaten, they talked for a while more. They discussed the meeting details and the speaking times. Bob was going to open the meeting, followed by John and after lunch Dan would share the vision to the group.

The next morning came quickly. It seemed that Dan's head had just hit the pillow when the alarm was ringing to wake him up. After a quick shower and getting dressed, he went down to the restaurant to eat with the others. "Good morning everyone," he said as he walked up to the table. John, Nikki, and Susan had already come back from the buffet table with their food and were beginning to eat.

"Good morning to you, too," replied Susan with a grin. She was really enjoying this trip and it was so good to be back in the flow of the ministry again. Ever since she had come back from the mission field, she had been full force into the business field. It was really refreshing and, of course, it helped having someone else to share things with.

"We were beginning to wonder if we were going to have to go up and knock on your door," said Nikki teasingly.

"I kind of lost track of the time in the shower," replied Dan. "I love a hot shower in the morning. It is a lot like having a steam bath. It awakens the senses and relaxes the muscles. Of course, it also helped having the Eucalyptus oil to stimulate my breathing. Wow! What is that? It sure smells good." Dan was looking directly at Susan's plate.

"It tastes good too," replied Susan. "You better get yours before it is all gone." She was having a good time ribbing him and she noticed that he was enjoying it too. It was good to see him so relaxed.

After Dan made it back to the table, John asked him, "So, how was your night?"

"Uneventful! In fact, I don't remember a thing," replied Dan. "Is everyone ready for today?"

"I am as ready as I will ever be," said John. "I have a rough outline in my mind of how I am going to lay the framework for you to share your vision. Just open your mouth and let Holy Spirit speak through you."

"Thanks," said Dan. "That really helps. Sometimes I find myself wondering what I need to share and which part goes where. I will follow your lead."

The meeting was about twice the size as Bob had expected. There were people and leaders from all over the city. He began the meeting with a prayer and then introduced John and Dan. He shared a story with the group and then handed the meeting over to John. Dan listened closely to his brother as he prepared the group for his vision. John was very eloquent with words. He shared with them about dreams and visions in the Bible and how God talks to His people. Soon it was time for lunch and they all went out to eat.

"So far, so good," said Dan, "no problems yet."

"Well, get prepared, because if you heard right, the fireworks will begin shortly," said Bob. "I'm not looking forward to this." He was really bothered by having to deal with a situation like this.

Dan walked over to the middle of the stage and began to speak. He didn't seem to have any problems sharing the vision. The trouble started when he was halfway through the explanation of it.

Suddenly, two men in the middle of the auditorium stood up. One was dressed in a white suit with a marine blue shirt. He looked like he was in his fifties and had just come right out of the TV show "Miami Vice." He yelled out, "How dare you come into our city with your lies. This vision is only meant to separate the Lord's people and bring despair. Who do you think you are? Have you ever been to seminary? What credentials do you have that give you the right to speak to us like this? You need to leave. People, don't listen to his lies. He …"

At that moment, two security guards began to remove the two from the assembly. Dan spoke up gently, "Sir, I don't know you, however you are surely welcome to your opinion."

Next, the guy who had stood up next to the one in white, turned and said to his comrade, "See, I told you! I told you that they wouldn't listen to you."

The guards quickly escorted the two outside of the auditorium as Dan continued, "I want you all to know, that I am not here to spread any lies. The things I am sharing are what I heard from the Lord and His angel. It is you who must decide if it is the truth. You are responsible for the choice you make concerning this message. I am only the messenger. It is my prayer that this message will bring His people closer together and bring the healing that is necessary for us to go forward in His grace and mercy." He could see that there were some people who were physically shaking by the outburst. "Will you join with me in prayer before I continue? Lord, we ask that you comfort everyone here and let your truth prevail." Dan then continued to share the remainder of his message. The rest of the meeting went without any more problems.

After the meeting, Bob came up to Dan and asked him if he would like to meet with some of the leaders of his group and some from other groups in the city. A group of leaders had approached Bob directly after the meeting and asked if they could all get together. Dan replied, "Sure Bob, that would be good. I could use some company right now."

John, Nikki, Susan and Dan joined the others in one of the conference rooms to discuss the meeting and the major interruption. The two men had become so irate and demonstrative that security had to escort them to their cars to leave the property.

Chapter 10

The Vision Unfolds

Bob began in all seriousness, "I want you all to know that this situation today was foretold. We did all we could to prevent it, but as you can see, it still had a bad effect on some of the people. The one thing we did not expect was the additional people who attended from other parts of the city. I guess word got out about the vision. I had originally planned this meeting for our group only. However, in the last couple of days I decided to open it up to others because the word got out and numerous requests were pouring in from others who wanted to attend. The purpose of our getting together is to hear anyone who has any concerns or direction concerning the meeting."

Tom, a recognized leader in the community, began to speak, "Dan, that is not all of the vision, is it?"

Dan was a little caught off guard, "No, actually it wasn't. As John was speaking this morning, I started to see more of it."

"That is what I thought," continued Tom with excitement. "I have known for a while that it was time for a new revelation to come to God's people. I believe this is it. I have noticed that over time, the Lord reveals a deeper understanding of His Word to his people. Can you share a little more with us?"

"Yes, I can," replied Dan. Tom's words really helped comfort him. "I was shown a path this morning that was blocked. No one could get through on this particular path. It was dark, overgrown and dangerous. It was then that I understood that this vision was to help remove the blockage."

Bob interrupted, "Dan is there a lot to this new part of the vision?"

Dan replied, "It will take a while to share it."

Bob continued, "Since it is getting close to dinner, how about we break for a while and meet back here around seven o'clock? Is this okay with everyone?"

Tom replied, "That sounds good to me. I am getting hungry. Do you mind if we invite others to come?"

Bob replied, "That will be fine. We can move to a bigger room. I will let the setup crew know."

Everyone else was in agreement too.

At dinner, Susan leaned over to Dan and asked, "How are you doing?"

"I am doing great," he replied. "This is really nice with the exception of the outburst today. I think I could do this full time. It is so exciting and rewarding. I like seeing people's lives change for the better. It is so much more fulfilling than the business world."

"I am really excited too," she stated. "I was really concerned when the two men stood up. I didn't know what was going to happen. I am so glad you are all right. How would you like to have a cup of tea together out on the terrace after the meeting?"

"I would really like that," replied Dan, his eyes beaming with love for Susan. "That would be an exceptionally wonderful way to end the evening."

As they walked into the meeting room, they were so amazed to see the crowd that had gathered on such a small notice. "Wow!" Dan exclaimed excitedly as he began to share the next phase of the vision. "I am deeply encouraged by seeing all of you here tonight. I really did not expect this. Thank you for your support."

"Thank you too!" a shout came from the crowd. Several more shouts of encouragement came and then the whole group started clapping. Some even stood to their feet.

After the noise had quieted down, Dan continued. "I am so blessed. I am so glad you were not hurt by the outburst earlier. It is not my intention to hurt anyone. I am here to simply share that which I receive. It is up to the Lord to touch your heart and to tell you of His plans for your life. I desire for each of you to be truly whole and be able to walk in the full destiny He has planned for you."

"I have been asked to share more of the vision tonight. This morning, as John was speaking, more of the vision was opened up to me. I began to see many paths on something that looked like a map, but it was like a hybrid map similar to the Google map. It was like looking at a satellite view of this particular area with a map outline layered over the top. Then only a certain part of this map came into view. This particular path was totally blocked and overgrown with vines and other kinds of plants. I asked the Lord about this and He replied,

'This is a path that has been covered over for a long time. Very few have journeyed down it, yet it is a path that is very important for my people, especially in this generation and at this particular time. Those who take the risk to open it up, walk down it and help others to walk on it, will be greatly blessed. Share this with those around you. This word will bring a dividing line to My people. Those who choose not to walk this path will soon see their works dry up. These are the ones who are more interested in building their own kingdoms for their own egos, rather than do the work I have sent them to do. Their works will come to nothing. I will not share My Glory with anyone else. Do not be deceived, this word will bring division. I have chosen to divide that which is mine from that which never was. The outburst, which will come later in

this meeting, will be tiny compared to that which is to come. If you choose to go this way, make a choice to not look back. Share My love with My people and remember, I Am with you.'"

An amazing hush came over the whole room as Dan finished the last words of the Lord. The atmosphere in the room had changed. There was a sense of awe, respect, honor and a tremendous fear of the Lord. It felt like the King had walked into the room and no one dared to interrupt. Every ear was attentive to every word Dan spoke. Dan began to get a little weak as he continued. "There are many leaders who are consumed with getting their names in the marquee lights. Their message is about prosperity, what you can get from the Lord and how you can manipulate scripture to get what you want. They have implemented many programs to keep people and their children satisfied and entertained. They are no different from the world in their seeking after financial riches at the expense of their people. The innocent are being trampled and pushed away while the greedy continue on their way."

"This will not continue. The Lord is going to expose this in front of the world. He has given them time to repent and to turn away from their wicked ways. The blood of innocent people is on their hands. He hears their cries and the bleeding of their hearts. They are promised healing, but are continually stabbed again and again. Who is going to stand up and bring healing? Who will stand up for those who are too weak to fight? Raise your hands if you have had enough."

Dan looked around the auditorium as almost every hand went up. "Look at those around you. I ask you. Do you know them? Who are they? What do they like? What do they do? Do you care about them? That is the message I have for you tonight. You must put aside all of your selfish wants and desires and start caring for your brothers and sisters. Until the world sees His people loving each other, they don't have much of a desire to get to know Who He is. The disciples were first called Christians by the world in Antioch because they were Christ-like. We are not like that. We call ourselves Christians. We have it the wrong way around. Oh boy, we can sure preach it loudly. We can even use the political arena, but until we are walking what we preach, it really doesn't matter nor make a difference. We can entertain people all day long, but if it doesn't change them, they still face the same things every night. Loneliness, despair, depression and those kinds of things are the enemies. Are we making a difference? Do you care?"

Dan continued in earnestness. The words were coming to his mind as fast as he could speak. "How do we do this? Where do we start? We start at the beginning. The early church met house to house. When they met together every ones needs were also met. They took turns sharing what the Lord put on their hearts. They prayed for each other. They took the TIME! Where there was need for repentance and forgiveness, they did. These kinds of meetings turned the world upside down. The Lord added to their numbers exponentially. It was their love that changed the world, not mere words. Are we ready? Are we willing? Can we put our hands to the plow and not look back?"

The meeting was becoming noisy. People were starting to understand how far the church had strayed from it true purpose. Dan was sensing that people were starting to join in on the emotions of it all so he started to go a different route. "Please hear me. Let's refocus for a moment. This is not about getting on a bandwagon or getting all caught up in emotions. This is about changing our way of life. It can only be done one person at a time. It is going to demand sacrifice. We are an entertainment culture. We have gotten used to the comforts of our society. Caring for people is going to change that. It is going to take time and commitment. We will have to get out of our comfort zones. Certain groups of people will hate you. They are the ones who think they are religious. They are the ones who are building their own kingdoms. But be of good cheer, for your names will be written in the Book of Life and you will hear the words, 'Well done, My good and faithful servant.'"

People were standing and shouting with Dan. They were clapping their hands. The atmosphere was electrified. The presence of the Lord was magnificent. It was all about Him. He was being lifted up and all of a sudden everyone began to worship the Lord. It was spontaneous. Some even said later that they saw angels all about. People started turning to each other and prayed for each other. Some even went to those they had judged and asked forgiveness. Healings were taking place. The meeting lasted for over three hours.

After a long while, Bob got up and addressed the meeting. "What a wonderful time." Everyone agreed. He looked over at Dan and asked, "Dan, can you come back tomorrow night?"

Dan looked over at Susan, John and Nikki who were already nodding their encouragement. "Sure, I would be honored."

"How would everyone like to meet back here at seven o'clock tomorrow evening?" he asked. It sounded like one mighty voice as they all agreed. "We will see you then. The Lord bless you all as you go on your way."

Bob pulled Dan aside and they went into another room to talk. "Dan, do you realize what is happening? This is a whole new move of the Lord. The time is right. This is the right message. I just want to thank you for coming. I don't know what is going to happen next, but I sure am excited. I have never seen so many people get touched in this way and the presence of the Lord is awesome. I am guessing we will have at least double the amount of people tomorrow, even on a Monday night. We have been praying for a long time for something like this. We, as leaders have spoken too many words without the power of the anointing. This is so refreshing."

Later, back at the hotel, Dan and Susan got together in a secluded area of the restaurant. "That was wonderful," Susan began. "It has been a long time since I have felt the anointing so strong. This is going to be powerful. When lives start changing like they did tonight, bigger miracles are not far behind." Susan leaned over and put her head on his shoulder. Dan put his arm around her shoulders and hugged her. "This feels really good. Thanks!" she added.

"You are quite welcome. I feel so much peace that I just want to stay in this moment forever," said Dan softly. His body had gone from weakness on the stage to feeling an awesome surge of strength and now it was coming back to normal. "That really takes a lot out of a person. I almost feel like a limp noodle. That was so amazing. I have seen a lot of things being around John, but never anything like this. Most of the time leaders will pray individually for people and they get healed or delivered, but to see the Sovereign hand of the Lord just take over a meeting is incredible."

"Yes it is," Susan added. "I am so proud of you in

a good sense. You are still yourself after all of that. There are some people who would have let that go to their head and try to take some of the credit. You are so special to me. I love you, Dan." Susan had looked up and was looking deep into his eyes as she said this.

Dan looked into her eyes also. He remembered the words Alex had spoken to him about her. "I love you too, Susan and I am so glad you are who you are too. I feel so honored that Father has put someone so special into my life. There are so many people out for themselves, so to find someone who wants to see His will done is priceless. Thank you for being you."

"You're welcome," she said with a grin. She edged closer to him and put her arm around his side as she squeezed. "I feel the same about you. There was a time in my life when I didn't think anything like this could ever happen to me. This just makes it that much better. What do you think will happen tomorrow?"

Dan replied, after thinking for a moment, "I don't know, but if it gets much better than this, I don't know what we are going to do. In my mind I am thinking, *'How can we top this?'* Yet, I know that this is only the beginning. I am expecting even more revelation as we share what we have been given."

Dan and Susan had walked up to their rooms and Dan was just about to leave Susan's door when they heard a voice from inside her room. "Come on in, Dan," insisted Alex. "There is something I need to show you both."

As they went into her room, it became engulfed with a light that seemed to come from everywhere. Alex was standing in the middle of the room. "Come over here. Do you see that over there?"

"Yes," they replied in unison.

"Tell me what you see," he began.

"It looks like a fortress," began Susan. "It is all shut up and secure."

Alex took them up above the fortress for a different view. "Now, what do you see?"

Dan replied, "It looks like what used to be a beautiful garden, but now it is overgrown with vines and thorns. The ground is all cracked and the ponds are all dry."

"It looks very dismal and depressing," added Susan.

Alex took them a little closer and asked them the same question as before.

Susan shouted in excitement, "I see a beautiful rose bush in the middle of the garden and it is blooming. It must be a miracle because there doesn't seem to be enough water to keep it alive."

"There is such a small clearing around it that it is totally hidden from view except to see it from above," added Dan.

"That is right," said Alex. "This is the result of

today. This garden was all shut up and desolate until today. No one cared for it. It once was so beautiful. The water was flowing and over there were waterfalls. The trees were lovely and the birds used to sing and flit around. People used to sit under the trees and the children would play. You have helped to bring life into it again."

"But what about the fortress, it still looks like it is all locked up. How can anyone get in?" asked Dan.

"They have already begun. Soon the fortress itself will be removed and people will come from everywhere to enjoy this garden," said Alex. He continued to share the story of the garden with them for most of the night.

It was very late when Dan finally got to his room. He had been overwhelmed by what he saw and heard. Alex had told them to share this vision with everyone at the next meeting. He hardly slept at all. His mind kept going over everything that was happening. He was not alone in this anymore. Now, Susan had seen Alex too. He began to wonder how far this was going to go.

The next day, Dan and Susan decided to spend some time alone and just walk around the city. It was good to relax and be with each other. They had a lot to talk about. They talked about the business, the ministry that was opening up and also about their relationship. They even talked about getting married, but wondered how everything was going to fit together. They decided to take everything one step at a time.

That evening the crowd had tripled in size. Bob had recorded the first two sessions and made the DVD's available to anyone who wanted them. Even though they had not taken or requested an offering, people were so appreciative that they had brought money up to the stage. The evening started off with worship. It was spontaneous. No one lead it at all. Everyone was singing their own song to the Lord, yet all the voices blended together into one magnificent song. It went on for a long time before they came to a time of silence.

After a long period of silence, Dan felt the urge to get up and speak.

Chapter 11

A New Garden

Dan began to share about the encounter the night before with Susan and Alex. He asked Susan to come up with him and they began to share the story together. They told how they had seen the different views of the garden and about the rose bush in the middle. Susan, being the artist she was, had sketched several pictures of the garden. They had scanned them into the computer and began to show them on the big screens as she described each one.

Then Dan began to share some of the things Alex had spoken. "Yesterday, this garden began to grow again. Love has started growing in it again. There is still much work to be done, but we can do it. This garden is to be a place for everyone to enjoy. It is not to be hidden and closed up anymore. It is for the healing of the nations. Now, I am going to explain its meaning."

"This garden was once a beautiful place where many people came and enjoyed. It was so great that it changed the nations. But over a period of time, fear crept in and many leaders felt the need to protect it themselves. They began to build walls around it and put up gates. They allowed seeds of fear, pride, envy, hatred, bitterness and the like to be planted in the midst of it. These vines and thorns grew up fast and soon used up all of the available water and the beautiful plants began to die from neglect and lack of water. Soon the garden was shut up tight and forgotten. This is what it looks like today."

They moved on to the next sketch that Susan made. "This is the next step in the garden. We must continue to work like we did yesterday. We must dig up the vines and thorns of fear, pride, envy, hatred, bitterness and jealousy. As we get rid of them in our individual lives, we can then get rid of them as a whole. The soil must be turned and watered again so that it is soft again. Then the new seeds that are planted will spring up and bring new beauty to the garden. The Lord will water it with His presence and cause His light to shine upon it. We need to dismantle the wall built by human hands and let the Lord be its Fortress. Then the garden will shine into the darkness and the whole world will see the glory of the Lord and come to it."

Dan stood back and Susan began to speak, "Beauty comes from the Lord. The Lord loves a cracked vessel. He can shine His light through those who have surrendered to Him and humbled themselves. If His leaders will dare to embrace this season and let go of their fears, He will come into their meetings and change many lives. The glory that was seen in the early church is nothing in comparison to what is beginning to happen now. Can you imagine no more divisions among His people? Can you imagine people who are not afraid to reach out in love and support each other? Can you imagine what will happen to the world when they can see the Church instead of hearing its noisy gong? What will happen when people are no longer being judged, but are accepted as they are? It is His place to change them."

Then Dan continued, "Can you see it? Even now some of you are starting to see visions and receive words from the Lord. The body must begin to function as the body. Can the foot do the job of the hand? Can the mouth see like the eye? No! Each of us must be satisfied and willing to fulfill the destiny we were designed to do. No one is higher than the other in the Kingdom of God. If you are a man, then be the man that God created you to be. If you are a woman, then be the woman God created you to be. Men and women must walk in harmony with each other. Let there be true examples of men and women so others may see the glory of the Lord. If you are a leader, then be the leader you were created to be. If you are a helper, then be the best at what you do. Leaders need to let go and give the Lord His place. Let Him be the Shepherd and stop getting in the way and quenching the moving of the Spirit. Each one of you will know what to do as you let Him show you. Only when you become the person you were created to be will you be truly free and satisfied. Only then will you experience true joy and peace. If you are walking down someone else's path, not only are you preventing them from their destiny but you are missing yours."

Susan then picked up where Dan left off. "Many of you are going to be starting businesses. God is going to give you the plans and even inventions, but you can not do it alone. Some of you have been given the gift of wealth, but it is not just for you. Some of you are prophetic and some of you have the gift to counsel. Everyone has their own special gifts. Each one of us must help the rest of the body. Selfishness has no place here. If you can not or will not do this, please leave now. This is a dangerous place to be. We are getting ready to enter the times of Annanias and Sapphira. Please, I beg you, do not lie to the Holy Spirit. You are free to make you own choices. You are free to keep your own possessions or to share or give them away. You are free to walk as close to the Lord as you desire, but be careful that you do not hurt any one of His people, nor stand in the way of His purposes. People are going to be coming in with all kinds of needs. There will be no place for pride, arrogance, unforgiveness and bitterness. Please let go of it now. Confess your sins to the Lord and let Him cleanse and forgive you. Be filled with His life."

"There has been much destruction to the earth. Many chemicals have been used in farming and the land has not been given rest. Scientists have developed many hybrids that are not nourishing our bodies," said Dan. "Some of you will be in charge of new farms that will raise new crops and others will work with raising pure animals for meat. There will be new businesses that will focus on helping people rather than just financial profit. Businesses that are built solely for profit will become a thing of the past. No one will buy their merchandise anymore. We need to be sure we take care of the widows, the orphans and the poor. Everyone has a place in His Kingdom."

Susan added, "There are so many who are going to come in that we are going to be real busy. There is a shaking going on in the heavenlies. It is beginning to be felt in the natural. Turn away from the distractions of life. Things are going to continue to get worse in the world. Do not be dismayed. Stay focused. The harvest is great but few are the workers. Concentrate, meditate and pray continually. Meet with and encourage each other. Use the tools of technology the Lord has given our generation to increase our ability to do more with less. Grow in His grace. Walk in His peace. Speak with His truth. Judge each other according to His mercy. Continue in His faith. Share His love and experience His life."

As they finished speaking, several people got up, walked up to the front and asked if they could share. Dan let each one of them share what they had seen and heard. People were being joined to each other. Relationships were developing. Some of the people had brought snacks and drinks for the meeting. They set up tables at the back and served. Great peace had settled among them and in their hearts. Each one had something to share and each one received.

A short while later, Bob walked up to the front to make some announcements. One of the announcements was that they were going to open the building 24/7 starting tomorrow for anyone to come in and use the facilities. "We will make available certain rooms for prayer, ministry and fellowship. We are going to open the kitchen area for those who like to cook and share in this area. We are going to add a free wireless internet connection. There will be meeting and conference rooms available to help with establishing new businesses. We have volunteers for child care. And we will set up other areas as the need arises. This building will become a source of family life."

After his announcement most of the area leaders

got together. Many of them stated they were going to do the same with their buildings. They also agreed to share the gifts and talents of their groups with the whole. A sense of destiny came upon them all as they began to realize the potential they possessed. The scripture had been there all along, but now it had become real. Some of the leaders met each other for the first time. For the first time, they saw each other as family instead of competitors.

Dan, Susan, John and Nikki met in the restaurant before turning in for the night. They were totally amazed at the events of the day. "This is miraculous," John began. "I have never seen people do this on such a large scale before. Do you realize that nothing is impossible for these people?"

Dan added, "I have had so many calls from the States from leaders asking us to come to their groups and share what we have been sharing here. People have gotten on the internet and emailed their friends all over the world. They have even gone outside to make phone calls. I believe we will have to leave soon."

"I agree," said Susan. "As much as I would like to stay, I remember Alex's words that we must share this vision with others."

"This has been a wonderful day," exclaimed Nikki. "I really needed this. I feel totally refreshed and energized. A good night's rest and I will be ready for the morning."

"She is right," said John. "We need to be wise during these times and make sure we rest when we have the opportunity. Some of these days are going to be very long and we need to listen when wisdom speaks."

"Well, okay! You convinced me," said Dan jokingly. "But seriously, I do agree. We will see you two in the morning."

The walls around the garden were coming down. A lot of the thorn bushes and the vines had been removed and thrown into the furnace. The hard ground had been broken up and watered. New seeds were being planted. The fire was beginning to spread, but in the distance another scheme was taking shape. Time was short and the darkness knew it had to move in quickly. It would be tonight while everyone was asleep.

Chapter 12

Attack In The Night

It seemed that Dan had just put his head down when the phone awakened him. It was Susan. "Dan, wake up. I need to talk to you. I am on my way over."

"Okay," he said as he jumped out of bed. "I'll unlock the door."

Susan must have run because she was at the door as he opened it. "What's up?" he asked quite concerned.

She had thrown her gown on and didn't even bother to fix her hair. It was all over the place. She looked totally frightened. "I just had a dream. Someone is at the building and they are planning to destroy it. Alex told me that we must intervene or we will lose the whole building."

Dan hugged her briefly as he tried to calm her down some. She was shaking all over. "You need to call Bob. I will be okay."

Dan grabbed his jacket and put it over her shoulders as she sat down in the lounger. Then he reached for the phone and dialed Bob's number. "Hello," said Bob as he answered the phone.

Dan immediately explained the situation to Bob.

Bob was really concerned, "I am going to call the police and then I will meet you at the building."

Dan hung up the phone and then called his brother and filled him in on the story. Dan got dressed quickly and then walked Susan back to her room and waited while she quickly got dressed. Then they met John and Nikki downstairs in the lobby. John had called for a cab and it was waiting for them outside.

As they got close they could see flames shooting through the roof at the back of the building. The fire trucks and police were already there. Bob and Cindy were out in front of the building with a few of their leaders. They were gathered around one of the front doors. It looked like some kind of sign was attached to it.

As they approached the group Bob looked back and saw them. "Hi mates."

"What is this?" asked John as he pointed to the sign that everyone was looking at.

"It is a warning," replied Bob. He was really angry and upset. "I can not believe someone would do this. The police are looking into it. The fire was deliberately set. Someone is afraid of what is going on here."

Just then the fire marshal came around the corner. "Bob, how are you doing?" he asked. The marshal, Sam, was a good friend of Bob's.

"Oh, just upset," Bob began. "I can not believe someone would do this. This is just not right."

"I know," Sam replied as he put his hand on his friend's shoulder. "The good news is that we caught it in time. Another five minutes and you might have lost the entire structure. The fire was very close to the natural gas lines. How did you know to call us when you did?"

Bob told Sam about Susan's dream.

"The Lord definitely intervened tonight," said Sam. It was then he saw the sign on the door. "I don't want anyone touching anything. It is possible we can get some prints and find those who are responsible for this."

The sign was made of poster board that had a message printed with a large permanent marker. It read, *"You have gone too far. Stop before it is too late! This is only the beginning. You have been warned!"* It was signed with some sort of insignia that they were not familiar with.

"What do you make of that?" asked Dan looking at Bob.

"I don't know," he replied. "I don't know of anyone who would want to do this, much less have the guts to do it." Cindy was embracing him to try to bring some comfort. She was in tears.

"What would you like us to do?" asked John.

"Nothing right now," Bob replied. "Well, maybe we can go over to the diner and get something to drink. I could really use the extra company right now. Thanks for meeting me here."

The whole group decided to go to the diner. They put several tables together and then sat down. The mood of the group was totally different than what it had been the evening before.

Finally Dan spoke up, "We really need to refocus. The Lord warned us of this and then he gave Susan the dream. I believe we need to be thankful. Like Sam told us, it could have been much worse."

Bob looked up, "You are absolutely right, Dan. This is His fight and it is also His building. Thank you, I needed to hear that. I want you four to know that I consider you my family. Everything we have is available to you. No matter where you are, we will be here for you. Personally, I would like to keep you around, but this vision must be shared with others."

"We were just talking about that before we turned in last evening," replied John. "We would like you and Cindy to come with us when you can. And by the way, we consider your group family too. I feel privileged to be a part of this. It is far more than I could have ever imagined."

After they had talked for a while and made sure everyone was okay, they prayed and then went back to their rooms. After they had awakened in the morning, they were glad they had turned in when they did. After breakfast they all went back over to the fellowship building. Much to their surprise, they saw a large group of people. The fire trucks were wrapping things up and several construction crews had arrived. It seemed that the word spread quickly. Several construction company owners had attended yesterday's meeting and decided they were going to get in quickly and make repairs to the building. Their crews were unloading equipment and supplies. There was also a group of people putting together a serving line. They had prepared the food in their mobile kitchens and were serving the workers. By the start of the meeting that evening, the building had been totally repaired and the roof sealed. All that was left was for the painters to come in and paint. They were also waiting on a few fixtures to be shipped that could not be found locally. The local news had broadcast a story about the fire and how everyone had come together to help. The building was so full that evening, that people had to stand outside. Those who could not get in for the meeting were given directions to the other meetings being held where they were setting up live feeds. All in all the attack served to increase the publicity and attendance of the meetings. The Lord was being Himself again, showing off His love for His people.

Dan and Susan shared the vision again and

it was broadcast live to the other meetings. This time the Lord walked into all of the meetings at the same time. His grace was there as each person opened their hearts and took care of their individual struggles. People saw visions and received healings and whatever they needed from Him. Forgiveness flowed freely and broken relationships were mended. The fire and warning were completely forgotten in the midst of the miraculous.

They were totally exhausted by the time they had gotten back to the hotel. They all briefly met again with Bob's group. The reports had come in from the other churches and the attendance last night was more than triple the previous night's attendance. Word was getting out quickly and the Lord was moving miraculously at every meeting. People were being touched sovereignly by Him. It was time for Dan and his group to return to the States, so they said their good-byes. Bob would be replaying the videos of Dan and Susan for their meetings. That night everyone had a good night's rest.

Chapter 13

A New Direction

The plane trip back was fairly uneventful. Dan was glad to be back home to normal, at least what had become normal. He had a sinking feeling though, that life as he knew it would never be normal again. He had really started to get wiped out on the trip. He was looking forward to another good night's rest. He had made plans to go in early to the office in the morning and get caught up on work. He steeped a cup of Chamomile tea to help him relax as he sat down in his recliner to do some reading. It didn't take long and he was ready to go to bed.

He had not been asleep long when a noise awakened him. Sitting up in bed, he waited to see if he could hear it again. It sounded like footsteps coming up the staircase. He arose quietly and headed to the hallway. Everything was dark with the exception of the moonlight shining in through the windows. Suddenly, he saw a shadow moving on the wall as the figure got closer to the top of the staircase. As the figure turned to face him, his stomach sank. There it was again.

"Terror!" he exclaimed as he started towards the once intimidating creature. A surge of energy was building up inside of him.

The creature took several steps back in amazement and fear. It was obvious that this was not the greeting he was expecting.

"What are you doing back in my house? I told you to leave!" Dan exclaimed with his voice raised and angry.

Terror began to tremble as he spoke with his raspy voice. "I have come to bring you a message."

"Oh, really!" taunted Dan, "and what makes you think I will believe anything you say?"

"Oh, you will," replied the creature trying desperately to be believable. "We are watching you and your friends. If you do not stop spreading these visions you will be sorry. There are more of us than you think."

"I know all about you and your friends," said Dan. "I also know who my friends are and there are more of them than there are of you, so if I were you I would leave now while there is still time for you to go and do not come back."

Suddenly the demon realized that this was not the same person he had met previously. Fear began to overtake the creature and in an instant he was gone.

'*Good riddance,*' thought Dan as he went back to

his room. *'Hopefully, I can get some sleep now.'* Just as he was about to drift off, the room suddenly was filled with light. "Welcome back, Alex. I can see that this is not going to be a good night for rest. What's up, my friend?"

Alex replied, "Actually, it is a very good night for rest. Every moment in His presence is all about rest. Be very careful that you do not put down your guard where the enemy is concerned. The enemy is a supernatural being and can see in the spiritual realm as well as in the natural, but you, however, can not. Don't let pride have any hold on you."

"I have come to bring you another message. Many opportunities are coming your way now. Some are from the Lord and some are schemes devised by your enemies to discredit you and your friends and bring you down. Don't look at these opportunities with your natural mind, but hear what the Lord is saying about each one," said Alex. "The message is being released to you in different segments. As you continue to spread the word, the attacks will also increase. The enemy knows that if you continue, his kingdom is going to suffer ruin. Therefore, know that he will do everything in his power to stop you. Do not take him lightly!"

Alex continued, "There are many groups that are going to want you and Susan to come and speak. Some will be famous and some you will not be familiar with at all. As you go to the ones that are chosen, a great attack will come against you, your business, and relationships from some of the groups that are rejected. These groups have hidden agendas, but they will be exposed to the whole world as they come against this message of the Kingdom. Some of these groups will be dismantled and come to nothing as they speak out against this new move of the Lord."

"I will do whatever He wants me to do. The main thing I want to do is to be pleasing to Him," began Dan. "I owe Him so much. I can never repay Him for what He has done for me. I will gladly do what He wants."

"This time it is not just about you," Alex said. "There will be a lot of lives affected by each decision you make. Are you able to handle that?"

"I don't know," replied Dan. "I haven't thought about it that way. I am all right with putting my life on the line, but it's different when I have to be responsible for others."

"You have to be alright with this. You can not take things personally. When someone speaks or acts against you, remember it is not personal," said Alex. "This fight is bigger than you. The attacks will be against the Lord Himself and you have to let Him handle them as He chooses. If you take these things upon yourself, you will be standing in His way. Stand back and let Him handle it, His way. Do you understand?"

"Yes, I do," Dan replied as He suddenly caught the revelation. A greater sense of the fear of the Lord touched him deep within.

"Your assignment is changing some. You are to start writing everything down concerning the vision. The Lord is going to personally give you the plans for new communities around the world. It is time for His body to come together. It is time to build now. He is beginning to send people to you with the same purpose. Your personal business will be redefined and broadened to establish new jobs and business opportunities for His people. It is time for His people to use the things they have been shown for such a time as this. It is time to bring in the harvest and to expose the lies of the enemy. The world needs to see the truth and a godly example," continued Alex as he pointed to certain areas of the previous vision. "This structure, that the Lord is building will suddenly appear in the natural. The ground work has been established in the spirit realm. It has been prophesied for years and now is the time for its fulfillment."

Dan awoke early the next morning feeling totally refreshed. It was just as Alex had said it would be. He was full of energy and excitement. He could hardly wait to get started. "Lord, You are truly amazing. I know I didn't do anything to deserve all of this, but thank You for choosing me. Thank You for Susan and everything You have given me." He felt the presence of the Lord as he had started to thank Him. He was feeling like he was on top of a mountain.

He pulled into his parking space as Susan entered the parking lot. She got out of her car with a spring in her step and a smile on her face. Her eyes beamed as she walked up to him. "Wow, I can see you have had a good morning too," she said.

"Yes, I have," Dan began. He continued to fill her in on what had happened during the night and morning.

Susan could hardly wait to share with him also. "I had such a wonderful morning too. I woke up with a song of praise and just started singing. The sun was shining through my window and I even heard a bird singing too. He was in the tree next to my bathroom. The room filled with His presence and it was just amazing. I wonder what is going to happen today?"

"I don't know, but we do need to be prepared for anything," Dan added.

"That is for sure," she continued. "Do you need any help with anything this morning? After all, it is our first day back in a week."

"As a matter of fact, I do need some help," said Dan. "There are some plans I want to start working on and I am going to need the whiteboards in the conference room. We need to go ahead and get everything set up in there. That is going to be our project room for right now. I also need your input and insight. I want to get John and Nikki involved too. I am going to call David later and have him start building out the extra space at the back of this building into a whole new section. This is going to be for the planning area of these new communities and businesses. I have a feeling that everything is going to start changing quickly. I believe the Lord has everyone in place already, it is only a matter of getting the relationships established."

"I know you are right about that," said Susan enthusiastically. "We have been in training for so long and now it is time to put it to good use. I am so excited for all of those we will meet. Hey, would you like some coffee and a whole grain fruit muffin?"

"That sounds great. I don't mind if I do," he said teasingly.

Susan came back to his office with a tray of food and two coffees. "Tonya stopped at the store this morning and got a snack tray along with some gourmet coffee. So here you are."

"This is great. Nuts and fruits are really good for me in the mornings," Dan began. "Thank you so much. You are so special and thoughtful. Sometimes I wonder if this is all real. I keep thinking I might wake up from a dream and it will all be gone."

"I will pinch you if you like, so you know for sure

you are not dreaming. I am definitely not a figment of your imagination," said Susan with a playful look on her face.

"I like that look," said Dan seriously. "You have brought so much joy to my life. I can't imagine not having known you."

"Thanks," she said as she leaned over to hug him. "You are special to me, too. I wish we could have met a long time ago, but then we would not be who we are now. This is the right place at the right time and I want to enjoy every minute of it."

"Me too," said Dan as he gently kissed her on the cheek. He looked down at his desk at the files he had been looking over. "It looks like we lost some of our clients last week. I guess news of Australia travels quickly. It seems that a few of them are concerned about our beliefs and the possible negative impact it will have on their business."

"That is a shame," added Susan. She was irritated by the fickleness of the corporate world. "It is too bad for them. The Lord is going to bless those who bless us. Well, one thing is for sure, that is going to give us more time to help our new clients."

"Now that is a good way to look at it," said Dan as he caught the depth of what she was saying. "I was just remembering what Alex said and I know that we are going to need extra time for planning these new strategies. Do you know what amazes me so much?"

"No, I don't." stated Susan as she looked at him intently, wondering if he was serious or just playing. "Okay, what?"

"It is the corporate world," Dan began. "When I look at how things continue to work out, I know that there is a God in heaven. The corporate world is always projecting the future based on what has happened in the past in order to determine what is going to happen next. By the grace of God this world system is still working. Any little thing can go wrong and totally devastate the world economy. Just think, we are getting the new plans from the Lord, Himself. We don't need to look at the past and try to figure things out. All we need to do is listen to Him. He knows what is going to happen next and furthermore, He is going to put the relationships together that we need."

"Plus, we don't have to spend as much money on research and advertising," said Susan as she began to have a deeper understanding. "It has always amazed me concerning corporate philosophy. They are always going after the new ideas after someone has already paid the price and done it, yet they squash most of these same ideas by individuals in their own companies."

"You are right," added Dan, "they are very greedy. It is all about making more money and they never stop to examine the cost. Many sell their own souls to the corporate world and lose their families in the process. What a terrible price to pay! If only they would take the time to see what is really going on. Hopefully, some will see what we are doing and want to change their lives and be free from the prison."

Chapter 14

The Net Starts To Form

Sharon knocked on the door frame as she entered, "It sounds like you two are having way too much fun in here. Dan, I have some new messages for you. I have been answering the phone constantly since I arrived this morning. The excitement is really starting to build. There are people calling from all over asking about you and Susan and also about the business."

"Well, it looks like we may have to hire an extra person to take care of this new area," Dan suggested to Sharon. "You have your hands full already and it wouldn't be right to put that extra burden on you. Are you up to training another person?"

"Sure," Sharon replied at the thought of having some extra responsibility. "I need to spread my wings a little and it will do me well to train someone."

"Of course, you know that will come with a pay raise," Dan said with a grin.

"Great!" she exclaimed as her eyes beamed with excitement. "That is always welcome."

"I thought you would like the sound of that," replied Dan. "You have earned it. You are a valuable person to us and don't you forget it, promise?"

"I think I can remember that," replied Sharon teasingly. "I promise."

"Susan can give you some names to call," suggested Dan. "We had a good response from our last hiring. Maybe we can find someone out of that list."

"I know just where it is," said Susan. "If you would like to follow me to my office, I will get them for you right now."

"Sure, that's great," said Sharon as she followed Susan to her office.

As Dan went through the names of those who had called that morning, he was astounded at some of the ones he recognized. "Oh Lord, I need your help. Some of these are very powerful people. I can see how things might not work so well if I were to tell some of them 'no' and refuse their invitation."

Dan picked up his phone and dialed his brother. "John, I need your help!"

"What's up?" John asked quickly. He had not expected a call from his brother this soon after the trip.

"I had another visitation last night with Alex," Dan began. "After I had arrived this morning, Sharon handed me a list of people who had called with invitations to speak at their churches, conferences and businesses. There are some very affluent people on this list." He also filled him in on Alex's message to him.

"I tell you what. I have some things to take care of right now, but I will get the prayer team involved on what we are doing and have them start praying," said John enthusiastically. "We definitely need to hear which direction we need to go in each situation. I will swing by the house and pick up Nikki and we will meet you after lunch."

"That sounds great. This whole thing is going faster than I can keep up with. I can use all the help I can get. I am already remodeling our offices to make room for the extra offices we will need to take care of all this new stuff," said Dan. "If this continues, we will have to open the third floor and build it out."

"I am so glad you bought that building when you did," said John. "I knew then you were not overbuying. It is nice to have that extra space available without having to do any major construction."

"That is for sure," said Dan as he thought about how his brother had persuaded him to buy this building. It had seemed too enormous for his small company at the time, but he was constantly adding more offices as his business had continued to expand. "I will see you after lunch then."

Dan and Susan worked the rest of the morning on moving things to the conference room and getting everything set up. All of his other workers were very busy on projects that needed their full attention. In a way, it had been a blessing to have some of his clients walk away. He really didn't have the extra time right now. Once they had everything semi-setup, Dan began to draw and write on the whiteboards. "Susan, we are going to have to hire another two people to help fill our places. We are going to have to let Tim and Marsha fill our spots and get these new people to train for their places. We have to make sure they have the same spirit and are trustworthy."

"I am sure the Lord will send us the right people," replied Susan seriously. "We probably need to ask John if he knows of anyone who would be able to fill these positions. Chances are that he already knows the right ones."

"You are so right," said Dan joyfully. "I had not even thought about that. I just talked to him a little while ago. By the way, he and Nikki will be by later. I thought I would get some of these things off of my mind and on the big boards so we can go over them later. I am starting to see how some of these projects need to be set up."

"That is good," she said with a grin. "I didn't expect for everything to start this fast. Have you thought about getting a prayer team together?"

"John is already doing that," Dan replied. "So far everything is going smoothly. We really need Father's word as to which invitations he wants us to accept. I am a little hesitant with this area. I wish it were someone else's responsibility."

"I understand that," she said as she started stacking the empty boxes. "There are a lot of things I would much rather someone else do and dealing with these kinds of relationships is at the top of that list. I am glad you are doing it and not me."

"Well, for your information, you are going to have some input into this also, smarty," he chided. "I was told by a particular being that I wouldn't be alone in this. In fact, someone was hand picked to help me."

"Oh, is that so?" she added. "What if I say no?"

"I think you would probably be in some trouble. I know I wouldn't go there if I were you," he said teasingly. "Don't you remember Jonah and the whale?"

"Who was that?" she said with a grin on her face.

"You know exactly who I'm talking about," he said as he hugged her.

"You know that I am not going to let you go now, bud," she said as she looked up directly into his eyes. "It took me way too long to find you and if you think you are going to lose me that fast, you are sadly mistaken."

"Now, that is what I like to hear," he began. "Someone who knows what they want and are committed to keeping it. I love you."

"I love you too," she said. "So when are we going to make this final?"

"I don't know," replied Dan. "Do you think we can fit it into our schedule?"

"We could always take care of it on one of our upcoming trips," suggested Susan.

"I hadn't thought of that," said Dan. "That would be great. What about Switzerland? I hear it is a wonderful place to have a wedding. We just need to make sure we take John and Nikki with us. I am sure he would be glad to do the honor."

"That would be very romantic," she said as she placed a scarf over her hair and pretended to walk in a gown. "I like that. Just to make it adventurous, we can get everything ready and when the right trip presents itself, we will be ready."

"I like that better," said Dan. "This is fun. Okay, let's get back to work. Oh, I'm sorry, we are. So where was I?" He grabbed a blue pen as he went back to the board and starting drawing the layout of the community. This was going to be a huge project.

Just then, there was a knock on the door and John and Nikki entered into the room. "It looks like you two are having way too much fun again," said John as he gave Susan a hug.

"You bet, and this is only the beginning," said Susan with a grin.

"And that isn't all," said Dan. "We are going to need you and Nikki to come with us on one of these trips."

"I thought we were going to be with you on most of your trips?" asked Nikki, jokingly. She figured that this was heading somewhere and wanted to be in on the fun.

"Well, the main reason we are asking is that we need someone to marry us," Susan replied with a sparkle in her eye.

"We are planning a nice romantic wedding on one of our trips. We will just take some time out in the midst of everything else, to have a wonderful time together," added Dan. "What do you say?"

John began, "Of course, you know we would be honored. Thank you for asking. Life with the Lord is always an adventure. I can hardly wait to see how this unfolds. I am sure it will be more than we can imagine."

"That is for sure," Nikki added excitedly. "I am so happy for you both." She went over to Susan and gave her a hug.

Just then another couple walked into the room behind John and Nikki.

"Dan and Susan, I want you to meet Roger and Jessica," John began as he turned to introduce the couple. "Roger and Jessica arrived two days ago from a mission trip over in Africa. They sold their business two years ago to go into the mission field. I told them about everything that has happened and they would like to help, so we brought them along to see how they might fit in."

After they had greeted each other, Dan looked at Roger and asked, "What made you come back at this particular time?"

"Jessica actually saw a vision and I had an angelic visitation," began Roger. "Her vision showed a map of the United States and an angel standing right on this area. He was calling out in a loud voice for others to come and help. That same night I saw an angel and he told me that our time in Africa was over for the moment. We would be using the relationships we had established there for this next move of the Spirit. The next morning we prayed together and then began to prepare for moving back to the U.S."

"Wow," said Susan, "what a story and I thought ours was pretty good."

"Oh, it is from what we hear," said Jessica. "John has filled us in on a few things and I would say you two are at the top of the list of incredible stories. We are just so thankful to be in on the work. All the things we have prayed for over the years and desires we have had are only now beginning to take place. It is such a wonderful time to be alive. The Lord is joining people together sovereignly and when they meet it is like they were always friends. This is exciting."

"It sure is but it is also terrifying," said Dan. "I am not so sure that I'm ready for all of this. Some of the people on these invitations are very powerful people."

"So is the One Who is sending us," said Roger. "We have seen some awesome things in Africa. Believe me, there are more who are with us than those who are against us. Be encouraged my friend, you are not alone in this."

"Thanks," said Dan. "I think this is the easiest project I have ever worked on. Everything and everyone is coming together. I hope it always works like this. I wonder if this is how it worked for Noah?"

Chapter 15

Business Incredible

Dan brought everyone up to speed on their new project. Roger's background was in construction and marketing while Jessica's was in advertising and design. It seemed like they were going to be a great asset to the project.

"So far, I have been working on the basics. We can expand and detail each section as necessary. I have started out where we are right now," Dan began as he pointed to his diagram on the first board. "It looks like we have begun right in the middle of everything. We have a basic business operational in our present office. Through John's ministry, we have a basic ministry organizational structure. As we get the project off of the ground, we will be buying an amount of land to house the community based project. We will be building this whole infrastructure from below the ground up starting with a power grid, sewer lines, gas lines, and water mains. Now, most of our electricity will be from green resources, but the whole grid will be connected to back-up generators. All piping will use the latest technology to ensure uninterrupted supply and safety. Every housing or office structure will be equipped with water purification systems to ensure everyone is getting pure water to drink, cook and bathe. We will have farmland located in a strategic area of the community and will use non-hybrid seeds, all organic fertilizers and organic pest deterrents. Everything we do must be in line with the scriptures. We can also use our gray water for irrigation."

"This is good stuff, Dan," said Roger. "I am aware of some new inventions in some of these fields and I know the owners personally. This is really exciting. Some of these people received these revelations years ago and are now ready to implement them."

"I know where there is some land on the northwest side of the city," John suggested. "There is an area specifically that would be great for farming. I know the realtor that has the listing. We should be able to get a good deal on it. It is far enough out in the country so we won't have to be concerned with meeting any city codes. What kind of time frame are we working with?"

"I am not for sure," replied Dan. "I am thinking as soon as we can. We need to check it out first to make sure it will work. Does anyone know of a surveyor?"

"I do," replied John. "I have someone in mind

that has the contacts to get most of the utilities up and running."

"That is wonderful," said Dan. "It looks like most of the preliminary work is all in order. I think we need to discuss these speaking invitations and find out which ones we need to accept."

"I have all the invitations listed and have made copies for everyone," said Susan. "How do we want to do this?"

They decided to join together and pray for wisdom concerning each invitation. After about an hour they had completed the task and gave the list to Sharon so that each could be contacted and a tentative meeting time could be scheduled. The afternoon went by quickly and soon it was six o'clock.

Jessica looked up at the clock and said, "Do you realize what time it is?"

"Wow," said Dan. "Time goes by fast when you're having fun. How about we all go over to Café Serena and get some dinner? We can relax by the stream and talk some more afterwards."

"That sounds wonderful," said Nikki. "I have been wanting to go back there since the last time we met there. It is so serene. They really named it correctly, ha ha."

"Alright, that settles it," said John. "We will see you all shortly."

Dan and Susan closed the office and then they

were on their way. It was an unseasonably warm evening, so it was going to be nice outside even this late in the evening. After everyone had eaten, they gathered the loungers around in a semi-circle and sat down facing the stream. "What a wonderful evening to cap off such an awesome day," said Dan. He had been watching the waterfall and was enjoying the sound of the water coming down over the rocks.

"That it is," added Susan. "It seems like we are on this huge train and it just keeps on going and speeding up. I am beginning to wonder if it will ever slow down."

"I know what you mean," said Roger. "I was thinking that myself. In Africa, everything we did was quite slow. Then we meet you and it is off to the races. I'm glad we had some time to rest before we climbed aboard. I have a feeling it will be a while before we see a break in the journey."

"I called my office on the way over here and found out we have some more invitations to sort through," said John. "It looks like travel is going to be really frequent. I think there were even some European requests this time."

"We will definitely have to take a look at those tomorrow," said Dan with a grin as he looked at Susan. "Maybe there is one from Switzerland."

Susan's eyes sparkled as hers met his. "That is just what I was thinking."

They spent the rest of the evening getting to know

each other better. Roger and Jessica shared their mission trip in Africa and Dan and Susan brought them up to date on their story.

The next morning found everyone together in the conference room. After spending some prayer time together, they went through the new invitations and checked off the ones they would attend. It was decided that Roger would be put in charge of the land development project and Jessica would share her time between the project and Dan's design company. She would be handling all the advertising and design for the project.

"I will talk with my friend and see if anything has been done with the land," said John.

"Great!" exclaimed Dan. "I am going to take care of the necessary details for the upcoming trips. I am going to have Sam devise a schedule to make sure the plane is kept in tip top shape."

"I will oversee the food and drinks area," volunteered Susan. "I know we will all want to have enough food available for those long trips."

"That is for sure," Nikki added with a smile. She had turned sideways and put her hand on her flat belly.

"Yeah, like you really have to watch what you eat," said John as he winked at his wife.

"We are going to have to develop a community

prototype that will work in different countries," Dan began seriously. "As the world economy degrades we will need to be ready. Many will fall through the cracks. We will need transportation and communications systems in place, as well as backup generators for all of the necessary equipment."

"This will be a model similar to the early church and the cities of refuge," added Susan. She and Dan had discussed a lot of these details in private. "The main difference between then and now will be the added businesses and local governing councils."

"That's right." Dan continued, "Some areas will need protection due to uprisings and catastrophes. We need to make sure we can distribute supplies as they are needed. There will be farms in strategic areas to supply food. We will also have water purification plants and portable systems available. Government agencies are going to be overwhelmed and that is where we come in. As the net grows, others will see the love of the Lord and come to Him."

Roger stood back in amazement. "I had not realized the impact these visions are going to have. Up until now, we have only seen things on a small scale. It looks like we are basically talking about another economic system functioning within the other, the Lord's economy."

"Well, like you said Susan, that's how it happened in the early church," added John. "They were under the Roman system of government and yet they were not only able to help each other, but the Lord was adding to their number."

"The revelation of the garden is really interesting," said Jessica. "The thing that amazes me the most is that finally the walls are going to come down. The Lord will protect the garden and those who want to come are welcome. They will all be able to experience His love and forgiveness. There will be healing for the nations and there will not be any more pushing and shoving. Those who are building their own kingdoms are simply going away."

AUTHOR'S COMMENTS

I finished writing this book in January, 2008 and have just realized the impact of this revelation in the Kingdom. I had first thought that I was only half finished with it when I stopped writing because I had so much work coming in at the time. It was only last month, after the Lord told me to start working on it again, that I realized it was finished back then, but was just waiting for the appointed time. Today is that day, July 21, 2010.

Well, at least I thought that was the appointed time. Now it is one year later, July 21, 2011 and it is being published. Another book, "Sentenced To Death, Destined For Life: Tell My People I Love Them! - The Janiece Turner-Hartmann Story" took precedence. We just finished publishing it and am going back to back with this one.

Habakkuk 2:1-2 NIV, "I will stand at my watch and station myself on the ramparts; I will look to see what he will say to me, and what answer I am to give to this complaint.
The Lord's Answer
2 Then the Lord replied: "Write down the revelation and make it plain on tablets so that a herald may run with it."

The revelation in this book is so awesome in the way that it was given to me in visions, images, and words as I sat at the computer and typed. If I remember correctly, it took less than six weeks to complete. I had forgotten most of the revelation over the last two and a half years and as I read through it again, I was amazed at how it is lining up with new prophecies I have been hearing lately. Only the Lord knows how this book will affect the lives of His people globally. I have put down on paper, that which I received from Him in visions, images and words. It is my hope and prayer that you are blessed by the contents and that your life will never be the same again. May you fly upon the wings of His wind and soar high above every circumstance and problem that would seek to keep you down. You were born for freedom and for such a time as this.

Joseph James

ABOUT THE AUTHOR

Joseph grew up in a small town in South Central Texas, USA in the sixties. He says he was fortunate to grow up in the country, because it helped him overcome the absence of his father. His father left his mother when he was three. Sometimes, he would walk for hours at a time as a child throughout the countryside in order to find peace and tranquility. He observed the animals in the wild and took note of how they lived and interacted. He also learned first hand about plants, farming, and ranching. It was during these times that He came to realize the Lord was real. Later in life, he would meditate on these precious times to help encourage himself, especially when living in the large cities of San Antonio and Dallas.

He is a passionate writer, singer/songwriter, actor and artist. He loves to create things and write stories that can help encourage others. He also writes in his blog on DestinyPathOfLife.com and Joseph-James.net when he can.

He understands what it is like to live in torn family relationships. He has had to lean totally on the Lord to help him make it through each day. He speaks directly from His relationship with the Lord.

Please feel free to visit his web sites at: ShaftOfLight. com and *DestinyPathOfLife.com*. If you would like to contact us, please send any correspondence to the address at the front of the book or use the contact form on any of these web sites.

Thank you for reading this book. We hope it has helped you in some way. Our goal is to help others, to encourage them and help them to find their destiny. There are several

tools available on the
Destiny web site. There is a
questionnaire available to
help determine one's talents
and gifts. There are also art
prints, books, music, and
some of Joseph's songs. He
is in his studio as often as
he can to record his music.
He has it on his YouTube
channel at YouTube.com/
user/jjhdestiny and on Bandcamp at josephjamesjj.
bandcamp.com.

May your life be blessed by the Lord. May you continue
to walk deeper and deeper with Him. May He become your
best friend. Rise above the things that would try to keep
you down and soar high above on His wings of love.

Join us in our new adventure and outreach,
GameChangers Universal. Keep up to date and see how
you can be a part of the "Follow Your Dreams!" Tour at
GameChangersUniversal.com and check out our new
online magazine, UnDaunted.

Books By
Joseph James

ISLANDS IN THE SEA: *SAGA*

ISLANDS IN THE SEA:
The King Walks In
Book 1

ISLANDS IN THE SEA:
The Lion Roars
Book 2

ISLANDS IN THE SEA:

Illegitimate?
Book 3

"Sentenced To Death,

Destined For Life:
Tell My People, I Love
Them"
The Janiece Turner-Hartmann
Story

"Destiny Path Of Life:

The Journey Begins"
An Allegory Of Life

Visit:

DestinyPathOfLife.com

&

SentencedToDeathDestinedForLife.com

for more and
updated information!

Special For You!

Be sure to visit our ***DestinyPathOfLife.com*** web site to download a desktop wallpaper of your choice for free.

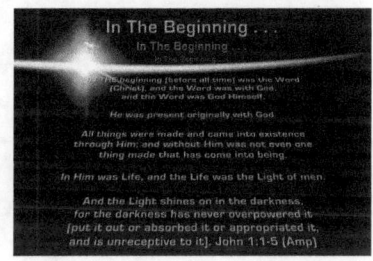

Visit *SentencedToDeathDestinedForLife.com* to read about a miraculous journey from a sentence of death to life of Janiece Turner-Hartmann, Joseph's wife. Subscribe to our blogs on both sites to keep up with the latest news and visit often for the newest additions and changes. Our main ministry site is ShaftOfLight.com.